WELL, I'LL BE DAMNED!

RICK TUBER

 FriesenPress

Suite 300 - 990 Fort St
Victoria, BC, V8V 3K2
Canada

www.friesenpress.com

ISBN
978-1-5255-7843-4 (Hardcover)
978-1-5255-7844-1 (Paperback)
978-1-5255-7845-8 (eBook)

1. FICTION, MYSTERY & DETECTIVE

Distributed to the trade by The Ingram Book Company

TABLE OF CONTENTS

Also by Rick Tuber

Just My F***ing Luck

Should Have Seen It Coming

Shanghai Cuts
A Hollywood Film Editor's
Misadventures in China

For Shirley-my wife, my best friend, my life. This is for you.

For Noga-I wish I could tell you how much
I miss you. Your smile lives in my heart.

For Stuart "*Would you like fries with that*" Rosenberg-
An amateur publicist and a 50 year friend.

1
WHAT COULD POSSIBLY GO WRONG?

Well, for Rick Potter a lot had gone wrong. Consider the mere fact that he currently found himself incarcerated in the California State Prison, Corcoran, or COR as it was known to its almost 3,900 male residents. It was just Rick's f***ing luck that both of his wives had been murdered and that a jury of his peers had the temerity to find him guilty of the second crime. A senior citizen and former Emmy Award winning film editor, now better known as inmate #739365, was serving a 30 years–to-life sentence for the recent brutal killing of his first wife, Tara.

He *had* seen her on the night she was murdered, and they *had* quarreled. In fact, she had hurled a Crystal cocktail glass like a Nolan Ryan fastball that had connected to Rick's cheek, sending rivulets of blood cascading onto her white shag carpet. And although Tara could be as cold as a block of ice, it was not his hand that had plunged an ice pick deep into her frosty heart. He had no clue who had.

The minimum-maximum security prison stood out like a medieval fortress in the Central California city of Corcoran, in Kings County. The ancestral home to the Yokut Native American people, the prison was located some 160 miles north of his former Northridge residence where his sons still lived. Celebrity slayers Charles Manson and Sirhan Sirhan had once called these barbed wire protected walls home.

Rick had adjusted to his new digs as well as he could. His cellmate, Nick Berresford, who was serving a ten-year stretch for masterminding a Ponzi scheme, had told him that time moves at a snail's pace in the slammer. A day seems like a week, a week like a year, and a year like an eternity. After four months behind bars, Rick could certainly vouch for that estimate.

The other members of his clique had nicknamed Nick '*Stretch*' because of his 6'5" slender frame. Stretch was in his mid-thirties, with a full head of curly brown hair and a boy-next-door look about him. He was in his second year at COR, and although he *had* scammed hundreds of people out of their life savings, he was really in prison because he had the unmitigated gall to confront Donald Trump about cheating on the golf course. The President took offense and had his Attorney General initiate an investigation. Before Nick could even collect his thoughts, he was tried, convicted, and deprived of playing golf for the next decade. One paid a steep price for standing up to a powerful charlatan.

Rick was fortunate to be placed in the minimum-security wing of the facility. The judge took his age and otherwise clean record into account and came to the conclusion that he posed no threat to himself or to other inmates. He also considered the older prisoner to be at great physical risk were he to be housed with hardened criminals.

So far, he was getting along fine with his cellmate and was philosophical about his current situation. He was here and would try to make the best of it. At 68, he carried more baggage than the

Kardashians on an extended vacation. Rick was of average height and had a head full of dark hair that was just starting to gray at his temples. His blue eyes sparkled despite his incarceration, giving him the appearance of a much younger man. He missed his family, single malt Scotch, and Shanghai, where he had been living for the past sixteen years. Life had been good to him in China, especially when drinking with his ex-pat buddy Bud, visiting weekly with his exotic masseuse Ming (whether he needed a massage or not), or distancing himself from memories that haunted him like a poltergeist. All were welcome diversions from a life that had fallen apart.

He had exiled himself to that foreign land shortly after his wife Cheryl had been murdered. Rick's daughter-in-law, Kendra, who had been convicted of the crime, had served seventeen years for the horrific offense. Over time, Rick had deduced that Kendra may have been innocent of Cheryl's murder, and that it was his recently deceased first wife Tara who had pulled the trigger with her perfectly manicured nails. Now, she was dead, too, and Rick was paying the price.

Messy as the whole affair was, Convict #739365 could survive if he had to. What choice did he have anyway? Sure, his lawyer Howard was working on an appeal and certainly was a likeable fellow. But Rick had about as much faith in the man's skills winning over a jury as he did in winning the lottery and being granted an early parole.

What bothered him most was that he had just started to connect with his six-year-old granddaughter, Noga. Now that connection had been irrevocably broken. Reading bedtime stories from a prison pay phone was not the same as watching her tender eyes drift off to sleep.

The ex film cutter had become quite popular among his cellblock neighbors. They enjoyed hearing Rick's stories of working in the film industry during the golden age of television, and he enjoyed reminiscing about halcyon days gone by.

A small group, made up of primarily white-collar criminals, was now gathered around Rick as he recounted one of those memories.

"It was around 1983, and I was an assistant editor for Aaron Spelling productions."

"Didn't that dude make *Charlie's Angels*?" asked his cellmate, Stretch.

"You're right. That was one of his many shows on the air at that time."

"That Farrah Fawcett had a great pair of tits," chimed in Randy Wiles. Randy was a short, bearded, early middle-aged man serving time for running a revenge porn website. He was nicknamed Porney for obvious reasons. He had an unhealthy obsession with the fairer sex, though he'd be deprived of their companionship for the next five years.

The men around him assented with a mixture of hoots, yelps, and catcalls, heartily agreeing with his assessment of the actress's body parts.

"Do you want to hear the story or not?"

The group assured him that they did.

"Okay then. It was a Friday morning, which was bagel day for the company. I picked out an onion bagel, smeared it with cream cheese, and got to work. It was my job to sync the picture to the sound for a show called *Matt Houston*. We were still cutting on actual film in those days."

"*Matt Houston*? Never heard of it," said Sol Moore, also known as Swindle. Swindle wore glasses with thick lenses and had worked as an accountant in a prominent firm. The young man had obsidian colored hair, dimples, a dour disposition, and three years remaining on an embezzlement rap. Like most of the others gathered around the old storyteller, he was too young to remember the show.

"Well, it was a private eye series and didn't last very long. Anyway, I'm eating my bagel and working away. At noon I delivered the reels to the projection booth to be screened. Usually, it was a small group that viewed the previous day's work, but on this particular day the room was overflowing. The precocious nine-year-old daughter of the boss was guest starring in the episode."

"Hey, that's Tori," announced Stretch. "She testified against me!"

"Nice gams on that one," added Porney.

Rick didn't think that Porney was anywhere near resolving his sexual issues. His rehabilitation could take a lifetime. It tended to take Rick quite some time to get through a story.

"So, Mr. Spelling arrives with a personal entourage of about a dozen or so executives and bodyguards. We're watching the footage and they were all very vocal in their admiration of the girl's performance. One junior producer called her a young Audrey Hepburn."

"Kiss-asses," intoned Sol the swindler.

"I'd pass on Tori," admitted Porney, although no one believed him.

Rick continued, "So, all of a sudden, long streaks appear on the film in the middle of her close up. The room goes nuts. Aaron wants to know if a camera has malfunctioned and if they'll need to reshoot. If the negative was damaged, it would cost thousands of dollars and wreak havoc with the production schedule. Spelling tells my editor, who was sound asleep before all the ruckus abruptly woke him up, to check with the lab right away—a task that he assigned to me. The crowd exited the screening room visibly upset. The director of photography started yelling at his camera operator, who in turn screamed at his assistant. One executive quipped that an Emmy nomination was in jeopardy. Just then it dawned on me what the problem was. I had accidentally smeared cream cheese all over the film. When I told my boss what I had done, he said, "Didn't hurt her performance any. Might have even improved it.""

The gathered convicts laughed as if they were free men. Their relish caught the attention of the ward's guard who headed over towards Rick's cell.

The men, heeding his glare, begrudgingly dispersed before the lights were extinguished.

2
CHEAP METAL HANGERS

Winter turned to spring, as it is inclined to do. The air was rife with the scent of orange blossoms and the sense of hope that comes with certain rituals, such as the return of the national pastime. Only in March do all 30 Major League Baseball teams, gathered in special places throughout Florida and Arizona, wax rhapsodic about endless possibilities and brim with equal self-assurance of winning it all.

But for baseball fan and retired Detective Sam Beetley, spring meant something else entirely. The scent of orange blossoms was the harbinger of allergies, and the season's sense of hope yielded to the heartache of past disappointments and the dread of facing even more of them.

The octogenarian remained in a coma, hooked up to several machines to keep him alive: if you could call such dependency living. Electrodes placed on his scalp were hooked up to an Electroencephalography (EEG) machine that measured his brain activity as discreetly as a no-holds-barred lie detector test. A plastic tube in his nostrils kept him supplied with oxygen. At first glance, one may have concluded he was asleep—or dead—but squiggly green lines displayed on a black monitor told another story.

Four months ago, while residing in an assisted living facility, the 85 year-old wheelchair-bound detective was working a case with the enthusiasm of a five-year-old playing T-ball. He was investigating the murder of Tara Potter-Conley-Finley-Goldblatt on his own, with no official authority. What else was a retired crime-fighter to do besides complain or join in a rousing game of bingo? Sam had reason to believe that the deceased's former husband, the convicted murderer Rick Potter, was innocent of the crime, and would be languishing in the crowbar hotel for someone else's evil deed. He had discovered a clue in the form of an ice-blue gum wrapper across the street from the crime scene. The unique wrapper had what appeared to be Russian lettering on it.

Sam wasn't surprised that the detectives assigned to the case had missed it. In his humble opinion, today's crime-fighters were not as thorough as they had been back in his day. Detectives Macfarlane and Morgan were considered '*minor leaguers*' in the department, and seemed more suited to handing out traffic citations than working murder cases.

Some months later, Sam had found identical wrappers in a courthouse ashtray and parking lot, where a jury of his peers had just found Rick Potter guilty of first-degree murder. While studying the people exiting the gallery for the gum chewer, Beetley espied a short, squat Peter Lorre look-alike with a mouth working overtime and followed him into the parking lot. Accompanying the man was Rosey Kern, whose daughter Kendra was married to Rick's son Nate, and was back in prison on another offense.

Sam had watched as the thick man opened a new stick of gum and tossed the wrapper to the pavement.

When the rather odd couple pulled out of the lot, Sam maneuvered out of his wheelchair to collect the wrapper. He placed it in an evidence bag, but collapsed after he shifted the valuable piece of litter into his shirt pocket. That was his last memory, and although he couldn't communicate, his mind continued to ruminate about the case. Why would these unusual wrappers appear at the crime scene *and* at the courthouse? Who was this odd little guy who looked like he belonged in a Humphrey Bogart film?

Sam hoped that the wrapper was still residing in his shirt that was hanging on a cheap metal hanger in a closet just four feet away.

Sam's health insurance was about to expire, and the need to make decisions about his protracted care was taking on a new urgency.

Doctor Doctorow was currently shining a light in Sam's dull eyes, surrounded by nurse Jennifer Mallett and hospital administrator James Coblenz.

"I don't see any change," announced Dr. Doctorow as he adjusted his black horn-rimmed glasses that contrasted nicely with his long ponytailed snowy hair. A stethoscope rested on a belly that had been expanding of late.

Administrator Coblenz checked his clipboard and said, "We can't keep him here any longer." Coblenz was a thin, vertically challenged man, who had the look of a boy who had been beaten up in school.

"But his EEG shows brain activity," insisted nurse Mallett. Jennifer was an attractive twenty-six year-old, with cascading brunette hair, eyes the color of a Robin's egg, and the cloying conviction of a faith healer. When she spoke, people tended to listen. "We can't give up on him now."

Sam *was* listening to every word. He tried to move, to say something—anything—but just couldn't. He felt as though he was in a coffin and dirt was being shoveled onto him in slow motion.

Coblenz wasn't swayed by the nurse's plea. Healthcare was a business, after all, and someone had to pay. "Sorry, but this old guy's a vegetable. We can transfer him to Chatsworth Care Rehabilitation Center. They should be able to take him for a few weeks. After that it's their problem." He left the room to attend to the business of moving the retired Detective to a new home—most likely his last.

Jen tried to appeal to the Doctor. "Couldn't we give him just a few more days? He seems like such a sweet man, and he's been fighting so hard."

"You have a good heart Jen, but Coblenz is right. We run a business here, and quite frankly, we need the space. Long-term care is rising to epidemic proportions and many patients have exceptional insurance *and* big bucks. My Mercedes doesn't pay for itself. *If* he does wake from his coma, I doubt that he'll ever walk again. And quite possibly never speak. Tough way for an old cop to go out, but that's life... and death."

The doctor exited the room softly singing a tune from *Frozen*. *"Let it go, let it go, let it go."*

Jen walked over to the patient and slipped a hand through his thinning white hair.

"I'm sorry."

She had a soft spot for law enforcement. Her father had been a man in blue for thirty-two years before an ambush extinguished his life like a firefighter putting out a brush fire. The young nurse walked to the closet and took out the clothes that were hanging on the lone hanger. She smelled them and made a face.

"I better wash these. You just might need them again." Jen closed the closet door and walked out of the room towards the laundry.

"No, no, no!" Sam screamed inside his head to an empty room that could not hear him. "Don't throw out that evidence bag!"

3
TSINGDAO BEER

"Shitfuck!" exclaimed Kendra Potter to no one in particular. She had just taken a handful of prison clothes out of an industrial dryer and had found most of the garments covered in blue streaks. This was not her first brush with a laundry malfunction and would not be her last. She had a habit of leaving magic markers in pants pockets, and the result this time was a collage of blue stains that resembled the Rorschach tests that she had taken and failed as a child. She thought the stain on one particular garment looked like a cow taking a particularly large dump. The other inmates weren't pleased either, when they saw their artlessly decorated clothing, courtesy of Kendra's carelessness. They were still women, for Pete's sake, and although their wardrobe was not on the stylish side, the blue stains tended to clash with their orange jumpsuits.

Kendra was serving her second stint in the Central California Women's Facility in Chowchilla, California; and this time it wasn't for a murder that she hadn't committed, but an eighteen-month stretch for larceny and parole violations. Attempting to steal jewelry off her mother-in-law's lifeless body was apparently frowned upon by law enforcement and society. So was bringing a weapon with her while she was on parole. She had gone to Tara's townhouse to seek some kind of retribution, believing that Tara had killed Cheryl and then framed her for the crime. She'd had seventeen years to come to that conclusion, but bad luck followed her like a storm chaser follows a tornado. And although CCWF provided inmate academic education, work and vocational training, counseling and special-ized programs designed for successful reintegration into society, participation was voluntary and Kendra was not the volunteer-ing type.

She placed the clothes back in the dryer and slowly slinked away. She was definitely not in a good mood—then again, Kendra was seldom in what most people would call a good mood. Prison was aging her, and her close-cropped hair was now streaked with silver. Laugh lines appeared daily on a face that never smiled.

*   *   *

Kendra's mother, Rosey Kern, was at her tavern getting ready for the lunch rush. Unlike her daughter, Rosey was a people person. Rosey's Tavern had become so popular that she no longer needed to toil in a hot and greasy kitchen. Her wide smile and easy manner reminded most customers of a friendly grandmother. She had a moon-shaped face, platinum hair, and was holding up pretty good for her sixty-one years.

Her son-in-law Nate was stationed behind the bar, muddling mint leaves into a jar like he had done for the last several years. He was used to living life without Kendra. Work, and caring for their son Jefferson, kept him busier than he liked. Jefferson, a high school senior, was getting by with his studies and Nate thought he had done a pretty good job raising him considering the boy's mother had been locked up virtually his entire life.

Rosey's live-in boyfriend, Ollie, sat on a barstool nursing a vodka martini. The Peter Lorre doppelganger felt pretty good about life these days. And why wouldn't he after getting away with murder? It was enough that he could enjoy his unfettered freedom, but the icing on the cake was the fact that Nate's father was serving the sentence meant for him.

The Russian national considered America's version of law enforcement as amateurish and no match for their Soviet-inspired counterparts. He pushed a wad of gum to one side of his mouth with a thick tongue and sucked an olive from a toothpick. Ollie spent most of his time on that very barstool, primarily because he had nothing else to do. The former Russian mobster was semi-retired and had a taste for spirits. Especially when they were free.

He watched his Rosey greet customers at the door, a function that she enjoyed and performed well. The restaurant was usually crowded, but on this Monday afternoon there were just a handful of customers enjoying a late lunch or early dinner: or 'linner' as she liked to call it.

Rosey walked over to a distinguished looking man at a far table and sat down. Ollie watched from his stool, wondering what they were talking about.

Nate noticed him noticing. "That guy's been coming in a lot lately. Drinks Tsingtao beer."

Ollie said nothing, but his eyes never left his Rosey. The guy she was talking to was now laughing out loud. Ollie was the jealous type, and kept a close eye on her, even though the man had to be in his seventies. He had an expensive haircut, a likeable face, and wore an out of style vest and shiny white shoes that appeared to glow.

Rosey smiled, got up from the chair, and walked to the bar. "Another Tsingtao for the gentleman, Nate."

Nate went to the cooler, pulled out a can of the Chinese suds, and poured it into a clear schooner.

"Who is he?" Ollie asked Rosey.

"Teddy Williams. He's in insurance."

"Not a bad hitter either," interjected Nate.

Rosey continued, "His office is just down the street, and what can I say, he loves the food."

"Is that all he loves?" grumbled Ollie.

She gave him a quick peck on the cheek. "Now, don't be jealous, comrade, it's strictly business." She grabbed the beer and returned to Teddy's table.

"Here you go, Hon."

"Ah, nectar of the Gods." Teddy hoisted the schooner in Rosey's direction. "To you, my dear."

Ollie kept his gaze on the insurance guy and chewed just a little bit harder.

4

THE ELEPHANT IN THE ROOM

Rick Potter's son Seth, his wife Boonsri, and their six-year-old daughter Noga were lounging on the Potter deck, which overlooked the San Fernando Valley. With them were Seth's older brother Paul and his girlfriend Madonna—both aspiring musicians—who also shared the large estate. The brothers were nursing a couple of bottles of amber ale, while Madonna was sipping a gin and tonic. Boonsri and Noga worked on tall glasses of homemade iced tea with lemon squeezed from their tree. They were finally getting a little relief from what had been a sweltering day.

The evening air had cooled, but wildfires had sprung up all over Southern California: a testament to climate change. When would the government take this seriously? That was the cosmic question of the evening. The group preoccupied itself with the subject that seemed to be at the very root of their discomfort.

Serenading them on outdoor speakers was the latest recording by Paul and Madonna.

"That's pretty good," said Seth, who was always supportive of his older brother's music.

"It rocks," said Noga as she started dancing with her Beach Barbie Doll, her wavy dark hair flying in all directions.

That was music to Paul's ears. He was a serious guitar player, and a songwriter reminiscent of the classic songs of the 60s. Madonna's instrument was her voice: a sound somewhere in between honey and wine. With her long blonde locks there was no doubt that she could be a star.

Paul took a long swig of beer and gazed at the distant mountains. The smell of fire filled the air. "Thanks. Needs a little tweaking, but we're pretty happy with it."

Paul was a perfectionist and was rarely satisfied with his work.

The conversation was interrupted by a mild zapping sound followed by a buzz-like sizzle, like a droplet of cooking oil on a hot stove. *ZZZZZZZZZZ* . . . followed by another shorter *ZZZZZ*.

"All right, got two more!" shouted Paul with the enthusiasm that could only come from a bug zapper electrocuting its prey.

"I've got four welts the size of quarters," added Madonna. The new Aedes strain of mosquitoes had infested the entire valley, leaving in its wake innumerable accounts of mean-looking splotches and excessive itching. It was like the city was under attack from distaff invaders from the Far East; specifically, members of a non-native insect species whose females seemed determined to bring disease and discomfort with every bite.

"Are they dead?" Noga asked her father.

Seth bent down and looked his daughter in the eyes. "Yes, pumpkin. They won't bite you anymore."

Noga squinted and thought before speaking. "I don't like that we killed them." She then bent to scratch the bites on her ankles. The adults had no reply to the child's words.

Madonna had been quiet for most of the afternoon, but at last decided to pipe up and address the elephant in the room. "So, when are we going to visit your dad?"

The tall, blue-eyed blonde had a point. In the four months since Rick had been incarcerated, his sons had yet to visit. It wasn't that they didn't want to; it was just that life continued, and making the three-hour journey each way would take up an entire day. They also rationalized that they wanted their dad to adjust to his new life behind bars before dealing with family.

"I guess it's time," said Seth. "He's probably as settled in as he's gonna get."

"I wanna go," said Noga.

ZZZZZZZZZZZZZZZZZZZZ. Another mosquito bit the dust.

Boonsri didn't think bringing Noga along was a good idea. "Wait until you get a little older, Nog. Grandpa's in a bad place."

"*Du farkirtst mir di yorn!*" exclaimed Noga, who stopped dancing and huffed her way into the house.

"What does that mean?" asked Madonna. Noga had a habit of speaking Yiddish, especially when she was upset. Her Thai mother, who had been adopted by an orthodox Jewish couple, was the only one who could translate. "It means you'll be the death of me."

The assembled group started laughing. They finished their drinks, scratched at bites, and decided that they would make the trek to COR on Saturday.

ZZZZZZZZZZZZZZZZ.

*   *   *

Rick Potter was holding court with his incarcerated cohorts; they were a captive audience after all. "So, I'm a reader," he told the usual suspects.

"I read magazines," said Porney, the revenge porn master.

"Isn't it difficult with the pages stuck together?" chimed in Stretch, the Ponzi schemer.

"Magazines are a thing of the past," added embezzler Swindle. "It's the digital age. People read phones, not paper."

"If I may be permitted to continue?" pleaded Rick.

"Go right ahead," interjected Stretch.

"So, I'm reading Joan Collins' autobiography, and—"

"Who?" asked Swindle.

"Joan Collins," answered Porney. "She was quite the looker back in the day. I used to whack off to her." His remark elicited groans from the group.

Rick tried to continue. "She was working on *Dynasty* at the time, and I was an apprentice editor on the show."

"Wasn't Linda Evans on that piece of shit?" asked Stretch. Rick affirmed that she was. "She lost a bundle on my investment venture. Most of my clientele were in the film business."

"Glad I didn't know you on the outside. Now, if I may continue. I wanted her to sign the book, so I brought it into work and waited for her to walk by. My room was near the *Dynasty* sound stage, and the cast would walk past our window on their way to and from the set. By the way, the *Dynasty* set had the best craft service on the lot. Their tuna salad was to die for. Anyway, I glanced out the window and saw her coming my way. I grabbed the book and a black sharpie and went out to intercept her. I introduced myself and told her that I was an editor on her show, and a big fan. For some reason that didn't impress her."

The assembled cons waited on his every word as Rick had their undivided attention.

"I held the book and pen in front of her and politely asked if she would sign it for me. She looked at me for a moment as if I had just farted. Finally, she snatched the book and marker out of my hands and scribbled her name on the facing page. I thought that was cool, even if I couldn't read her signature, but she turned and stared at me with eyes that could kill. She then slowly lifted up her left hand to show me that the marker had accidentally made a streak of black from her thumb to her wrist. She glared at me as if I had asked for a loan. It wasn't my fault, but obviously she was pissed."

"Damn diva," said Porney. "She deserved it." While the other listeners voiced their agreement a massive form dressed as a prison guard came over to the group.

"Potter, Warden wants to see you." That brought oohs and aahs from the assemblage.

Turnkey Harry Hinkle was a no-nonsense type of guy who didn't engage with the prisoners unless he had to. He looked more like a mountain than a man. His blonde hair was cut short and revealed a two-inch scar on his scalp in the shape of a question mark. A crooked nose and a cauliflower ear suggested a prior career as a boxer. By all appearances, he hadn't been successful.

"What for?" asked a defensive Rick. "I haven't done anything wrong."

"How the fuck should I know?"

The storyteller followed the six foot five inches of muscle down the corridor to the elevator.

"This isn't good, the poor fuck," said Swindle. He had been in the joint the longest and knew that a trip to the warden's office was like being sent to the school principle. Nothing good could come from it. The others agreed.

"I've got some stories I could tell you," announced Porney. With that, the others walked out of the room.

"Guys . . . Guys?"

Rick and the giant guard rode the elevator that smelled of sweat and broken dreams down to the first floor and waited for the steel bars to open. Within seconds, the barrier parted like an iron red sea. Rick recognized the rolling metal sound from the numerous prison episodes he had edited over the years. It was a sound effect that always made him wince. Now he was experiencing it live. He walked two steps in front of Hinkle like a sailor on a gangplank. A few minutes later, the guard stopped in front of wooden double doors and knocked.

"C'mon in," said a female voice. Rick hadn't heard a feminine utterance in quite a while, and the sound of it made him sad. He was a romantic at heart and knew that part of his life was over. He never remarried after Cheryl's death: no one could ever replace her.

Rick and Hinkle entered the warden's outer office and stepped towards an Asian woman sitting behind a desk that seemed too large for her delicate frame.

A nameplate on her desk identified her as Zoe Lee. She was striking in a mature manner, and appeared to be in her forties. She had shoulder length black hair that contrasted nicely with her porcelain skin. Fine lines around her mouth and almond eyes cast a shadow of hope. Rick couldn't take his eyes off her.

Zoe looked up and smiled. "Go on in, Warden Goldberg is waiting."

"Ni hao," said Rick using the Mandarin word for hello.

Zoe returned the greeting. "Annyeonghaseyo . . . I'm Korean, not Chinese."

Rick felt embarrassed. "I'm so sorry. Please forgive me."

"No worries. Happens all the time. You better go in now."

The uniformed mountain escorted the prisoner in and returned to the outer office.

Rick eyed the man who was in control of the rest of his life. He wore a tan suit with a skinny green tie and had a head of thinning gray hair that resembled a well-worn carpet. He had an air of confidence about him that fit his position. Rick guessed the warden to be in his mid-fifties.

Goldberg finished writing, looked up at Rick, and smiled. "So, how are you getting along?"

"Well, I haven't been raped yet."

"That's a good thing. We frown on that kind of behavior."

"Glad to hear it. I would like to see more nutritious options in the mess hall . . . Just saying."

The warden glanced up at Rick like he just wet his pants. "Well, *that's* not going to happen. So, I bet you're wondering why I asked to see you."

"It did cross my mind."

"I understand you were a film editor on the outside. In fact you won an Emmy Award."

"Guilty of that. It sounds like you've been talking to my agent, but I gave up editing years ago. And while we're chatting, Warden, I'd like to take this opportunity to mention that I'm innocent of murder. I wasn't fond of my ex-wife, but for God's sake, I wouldn't kill her. I get queasy at the sight of blood."

Warden Goldberg's practiced frown had heard that one before. "That's not my department. You're here now and that's not likely to change anytime soon. Not for about thirty more years anyway." He smiled like he had just closed a deal on a time-share in Sri Lanka.

"Let me get straight to the point. My grandson is getting bar mitzvah'ed and I'd like to put together a twenty-minute video for the ceremony. You know, old pictures and film clips of his life up to this point. An epic tale of his journey from boyhood to manhood."

Rick knew how to do these kinds of projects all too well. His son Nate had requested a similar video for his wedding and that had turned out to be a disaster. The guests' applause had confirmed that the video had been well received; however his new daughter-in-law, the ever-volatile Kendra, felt that her privacy had been violated. She threw a tantrum and flung the video disc down the hill like a Frisbee. Rick wanted to dodge this bullet if he could figure out a tactful manner to do so.

"I used to cut dramatic television. You should be looking for a 'reality' editor. I'm sure you could find several of *them* in here."

"There are currently *eleven* of them here, but Sonny deserves an award winner."

"I'm sure he does, but . . ."

The warden cut him off. "I have all the materials right here." He pointed a thick finger to a handful of boxes crammed with miscellaneous photos albums, old VHS tapes, and audio cassettes. "I just need somebody to sort it out and put it together in some sort of order. It shouldn't take more than a couple of days or so."

Rick's heart sank. He knew from experience that a project like this could take weeks of brain-torturing labor. His reticence was not lost on the warden. He swung the heels of his highly polished wingtips atop his desk. "Don't worry. You don't have to do this, if it's too much trouble. I am only asking politely for your help. But keep in mind that I can make your stay here easy or hard. Believe me, you don't want hard."

This was one time Rick wished he *had* an agent to negotiate for him.

"Any chance you could slip me a little Scotch while I work? It helps with my creative process." He knew that what he was asking for was almost out of the question, but what the hell, if there were ever a more textbook opportunity to float the idea of a quid pro quo—here it was.

Like Louis B. Mayer swinging a multi-million dollar deal in the Golden Age of Hollywood, the warden removed his shoes from atop the desk and stood up. His lips tightened and his eyes locked onto Rick's. "If you do a good job on this video, I can make that happen."

Sealing the deal, Rick tried to suppress his grin.

The warden tried his best to smile. "How much time will you need?"

"Depending on the nature of the material, a project like this could take a couple of months."

The warden shook his head. "The bar mitzvah's in three weeks. I'll set up a private room for you to work in. Just tell Zoe out there what equipment you'll need." He looked pointedly at Rick. "And don't breathe a word of this to anyone."

Rick understood. "What happens in the prison cutting room stays in the prison cutting room."

Warden Goldberg extended a soft hand to his inmate/editor and then ushered him out of the office. He gave Zoe a list of equipment he would need, never taking his eyes off her. She looked angelic and out of place in the cramped prison office. He felt movement in his pants and felt sad again. He didn't know if he believed in love at first sight, but Zoe came as close to arousing that feeling as anyone had in years.

Was it his imagination, or was she returning his gaze?

5

I GOTTA GET OUT OF THIS PLACE

Kendra's son Bryan, his wife Mona, and their daughter Abby were gathered around the breakfast table nibbling on assorted fruit and toast. Bryan wore a blue blazer and matching tie, while Mona was dressed in a fashionable tweed skirt and contrasting blouse. Both worked together in real estate and dressed for success.

Seventeen-year-old Abby was attired in jeans and a faded Nirvana tee shirt. Dress codes in her high school had all but disappeared. The lanky, straight-A senior was the star of her basketball team and popular with classmates.

Mona asked Abby if she would be home for dinner.

"Have to work after school, but I'm off at eight."

"I'll leave dinner in the fridge."

Abby had recently secured a part time job at the Chatsworth Care Rehabilitation Center, an entry-level position that she had hoped would be a prelude to a full-time career in health care.

Her dream was to play professional basketball, but she knew that making it in the WNBA was a long shot. At 5' 9" she was considered small for the sport. If she couldn't make three-pointers for a living, it was her wish to become a doctor or nurse. Catering to the patients was a good learning process, even if it meant emptying bedpans and changing adult diapers.

Bryan asked, "How's work going?"

"I love it. I try to interact with the patients as much as I can. You'd be amazed at how a little personal attention helps." She enjoyed working in the different wards, but preferred the comatose unit the best. Those patients never complained. Furthermore, she found the whole idea of people in a kind of limbo fascinating. They seemed to float between life and death.

Bryan smiled fondly at his daughter, proud of how she had turned out. "We'd better get going," he quipped before setting his coffee cup on the kitchen counter and picking up his briefcase. Mona collected the plates and placed them in the sink.

She gave Abby a quick hug. "Bye honey, stay safe."

"I'm right behind you guys. Have a good one, and sell some houses."

* * *

While her father-in-law, Rick Potter, was adjusting to prison life, Kendra most definitely was not. This time around was torture for the volatile inmate with undiagnosed mental disorders. Several of her fellow jailbirds remembered her from her first stay at Chowchilla and were not surprised to see her return. Kendra was as unpopular in the joint as she was on the outside, and she had only one friend: a scraggly thirty-two-year-old unsuccessful shoplifter named June. The wispy-haired former addict had her own mental health issues to deal with, but like the follower she was, looked up to Kendra.

Kendra sat alone picking at a hard-boiled egg in a crowed mess hall jammed with disgruntled female inmates, many of them clad in similarly blue-streaked orange jump suits. She had already lost ten pounds and would continue to lose weight like a fashion model days before a runway appearance. Perhaps with this latest laundry blunder, she could get transferred to a better job: although she believed that there was something very wrong about having to work in prison. She had about thirteen months left on her sentence that might as well have been thirteen years. She wasn't sure that she would be able to endure it that long. Thoughts of escape occupied her mind, but she could not come up with a realistic plan. Kendra was many things, but not really a criminal in the true sense. She was more of an opportunist, and that was what had landed her behind bars.

There had been a handful of successful escapes from CCWF, the most recent of which took place two years ago. They had all been accomplished with teamwork, and Kendra's team of two was no Houdini act. She had already served seventeen years for a murder she didn't commit, and now had returned for an additional eighteen months for simply trying to remove a ring from her dead bitch of a mother-in-law's finger. Eighteen months for that? Are you kidding me, Smalls? Where was the justice? She said "shitfuck" out loud and took a bite of egg.

June came over to Kendra's table carrying a tray containing something that resembled mashed potatoes. "Hey K."

Kendra looked up at her only friend and said, "That looks worse than my egg."

June smiled. "They must have messed up my order. I asked for filet mignon with a side of asparagus."

Kendra wasn't amused. "The food in this hell hole is shit. I hate this place."

"It's prison, you're supposed to hate it." June scooped up a spoon full of mush and deposited it in her mouth. "You just have a little more than a year to go. I'm stuck here for seven."

"Just your fucking luck. I gotta get out of this place."

June lifted her head and said, "If you can figure a way out, I'm in."

6
BAR MITZVAH BLUES

The ambulance pulled up to the nondescript three-story structure at 2:00 p.m. Nurse Mallett parked in a nearby spot, collected her former patient's clothing, and walked toward the ambulance where a pair of EMT's were maneuvering Sam Beetley onto a wheeled gurney. She followed them through the double glass doors to the first door on the left. It was marked '*ADMINISTRATION*,' and Jen was all too familiar with this particular office. This was where her care ended and the system took over.

The woman in charge, Letty O'Reily, was fifty-something, with lengthy graying hair that had once been coal black, and a figure that was hanging on to its youth. Dimpled cheeks made her look like she was always smiling. Nurse Mallett handed Letty some official looking documents and said, "Please take care of him. I don't think he's a lost cause."

"We take care of everyone here at Chatsworth Care." She quickly scrawled her signature, officially accepting one Samuel E. Beetley into her care.

"I meant no disrespect . . . It's just . . . I don't know. I have a feeling about this guy. I understand he was a brilliant detective back in the day. It's so sad to see him end up like this."

Letty smiled as she handed a receipt to the nurse. She put a hand on the young girl's shoulder. "I promise you, we'll take very good care of him."

Jen smiled, wanting to believe her. "I'll come by every now and then to check on him, if you don't mind."

But she was talking to air—air that smelled of antiseptic and old age. Jen was out the door when Letty used the PA system to summon staff to escort the new arrival to his quarters. Sam couldn't communicate or move, but was vaguely aware that he had left the hospital for a new home.

An enormous man of Samoan heritage and a Filipino dude about half his size wheeled the gurney through corridors of light green and lemon, stopping at an elevator. They pushed a button marked "3" and began their ascent towards the penthouse. The men steered the gurney to the right, eventually stopping at room number 305E, and opened the door.

All of the rooms in B ward were designed for double occupancy, but the person who would have been Sam's roommate, a Mr. Elwood Fry, had expired the day before. There was the faintest odor of death in the air. The average length of a patient's stay in Chatsworth Care was four months, but for some, like Mr. Fry, it was their last address. Others progressed enough to move back home, or to an assisted living facility. Sam would have the room to himself, at least for the time being.

The orderlies wheeled Sam into the room and gently lifted the old detective onto a bed covered with an air mattress. This would help prevent decubitus ulcers from developing. The huge Samoan was surprisingly tender, adjusting the pillows beneath Sam's head and smoothing out the sheets. His partner placed the new arrival's shirt and pants, which were neatly resting on hangers, into the closet. The Samoan turned on a lamp, and picked up the remote.

"I don't know if you can watch or hear this my friend, but it may keep you company."

Sam was silently grateful for having the television on, but an old episode of the original *Magnum P.I.* got him thinking about Rick Potter and the man with the blue gum wrapper.

His recent recollections had been expunged from somewhere inside his brain, but earlier memories were alive and well. He remembered the last conversation he had with Potter in his cell. The man had professed his innocence and Sam had believed him. As lead detective on his first wife's murder trial, he had been haunted by the look on Cheryl's face. Her green eyes had sparkled like flawless emeralds.

Potter had an airtight alibi, but had doubts that Kendra could really have committed the crime. Sam was swayed and eventually came to the same conclusion, but circumstantial evidence and an aggressive prosecutor had sent her away anyway.

Potter had told him that Tara's murder was a horrible coincidence. The odds of both his wives succumbing to the same ugly fate had to be astronomical, but things like this have happened. It was what made life so unpredictable. This time Rick had no alibi. In fact, he had been at Tara's the night of the murder; there was no doubt about it—but he didn't kill her.

Sam had looked him in the eyes and seen truth. He had decided to snoop around and that is when he discovered the peculiar wrapper near the crime scene. He had later found similar blue wrappers outside the courthouse. *Blue wrappers with Russian lettering.* He hoped against hope that it was still in his shirt pocket. It was not out of the realm of possibility that some well-meaning attendant had thrown it out with the trash.

Sam sank into a deep depression behind his closed lids.

* * *

Rick Potter was in a kind of solitary confinement of his own choosing. He found himself in one of the larger cells, surrounded by five large cardboard boxes that contained hundreds of photos and DVDs of a plump curly-haired boy named Sonny who was about to become a man.

The warden's grandson reminded Rick of his eldest child, Nate. In earlier days he had always enjoyed a good relationship with his son, but all that changed when Kendra and her juvenile delinquent son Bryan moved in. That nightmare had ended in Cheryl's murder and Kendra's arrest.

If that wasn't bad enough, Nate had the nerve to ask his dad for money to retain a lawyer for Kendra's defense, which Rick flatly refused. He doubted that any amount of time could bridge the emotional gap that now existed between father and son.

Rick picked up a box, took a deep breath, and started to go through the various images of a young life forever preserved in time. He would sort the photographs by years as best as he could, starting with the baby pictures and working his way up. He was grateful that this was just a bar mitzvah video that would stop at thirteen years of age. A wedding video would no doubt have had twice as much material to work with, and a memorial video would have encompassed a lifetime. Rick should know; he'd assembled both of those.

A fifteen or twenty-minute video would require hours of scanning and editing, but if there was one thing that Rick had plenty of, it was time. In a way he was grateful to be working on a project again; even if it was a home video for a teenager he had never met. Time passed quickly when he was doing the thing he loved, and he would give this video the same care as he would a network show.

He was seated at a long rectangular table where a printer, computer, and 20-inch monitor resided. The latest version of an Avid editing program had been downloaded onto the latest model Mac. It was a sad approximation of the elaborately endowed setups from his studio days, where dual high-def monitors, 100-terabyte storage towers, adjustable workbenches, and ergonomically designed chairs were *de rigueur*. He reflected wistfully on a time when studios and post-production heads pampered their prized editors with state-of-art equipment, luxuriant appointments, and even the occasional perk, such as the golf cart that was parked outside his cutting room for shuttling back and forth for screenings. What now lay before him paled by comparison, but it was more than he would have expected under the circumstances, and he was grateful to have it. He had spent more time at work than he had with his family—something that still bothered him today.

A small refrigerator stocked with soft drinks and sandwiches had been placed in a corner for when the editor needed nourishment. Rick took out a coke, popped the tab, and got to work. He had much to do and a short amount of time to get it done. He thought of the Scotch that would be his reward, and of Zoe, the warden's secretary.

There was something about her.

* * *

Paul and Seth were an hour into their three-hour journey to see their dad at the Corcoran State Prison. Seth sprawled comfortably in the back seat of his aging Honda, with Paul at the wheel and his girlfriend Madonna riding shotgun.

Noga had argued like a litigator to come along. It had taken a while for the girl to warm up to her grandfather, but when she finally did, it was with all her heart.

But her father had firmly refused. He had explained to her that visiting prisons was not for little girls. "There are a lot of bad men in prison, Honey."

"But Grandpa's not a bad man," she had argued. She had him there. When he promised her lunch at Weiler's Deli, she finally relented. While most kids her age would have preferred Chuck E. Cheese, or perhaps McDonald's, Noga was an old spirit trapped in a child's body, with an unusual fondness for Reuben sandwiches smothered with dark mustard and sauerkraut.

"So, did you let him know we're coming?" asked Paul.

Seth smirked. "No, but I'm pretty sure that he'll be there."

"God, I don't know how he can stand it," interjected Madonna. "He's innocent and this place will eat him alive."

Seth nodded his head. "Unless someone can find out who did do it, there's not much anybody can do."

Paul thought about this as his foot pressed down harder on the accelerator.

The radio was tuned to an alternative radio station as the car sped past miles of farms growing almonds, apples, and a variety of vegetables. Signs about the cost of water in the years-long drought dotted the landscape. Others warned of the impending Apocalypse, urging passing motorists to repent for their sins. It appeared that everyone had their own problems to deal with.

7

SEND IN THE CLOWNS

Abby left school at precisely 2:30 and made her way to the student parking lot. There was a waft of cigarette smoke drifting in the air like stratocumulus clouds. It was a proven fact that smoking tobacco led to lung cancer, chronic bronchitis, and emphysema, but her high school classmates didn't seem to get the message that the surgeon general had been preaching for decades. She jumped into her electric-blue Hyundai Santa Fe and wound her way to Chatsworth Care.

She pulled into the reserved intern parking spot, which was the farthest away from the facility. An employee here would have to work one's way up the corporate ladder to achieve better parking accommodations. She greeted a handful of residents who were gathered by the entrance hoping for visitors. They were always disappointed.

Abby found her way to the employee locker room where she changed into the pale blue uniform of an attending aide, brushed her long, russet-colored locks, and studied her image in the mirror.

She had peach perfect skin, eyes the shade of blue jays, and a slightly upturned nose. Abby thought she was more 'cute' than pretty, but a platoon of male schoolmates would have strongly disagreed with her assessment.

She maneuvered to the administration office to check in with her supervisor, Letty O'Riley.

"Hi, Abby. There's a new patient in 305E. Check on him first and make sure he's comfortable. Then you can work the rest of the third floor."

"Be happy to," Abby replied. Letty loved her energy and positive attitude. This girl would go far in whatever direction she chose to navigate.

The first thing Abby noticed was that the door to 305E was closed. She understood that it probably didn't matter to the patient, but Abby believed an open door was more stimulating to the senses. Also, the activity in the hall and the florescent lighting just made it seem less lonely.

She opened the door and peeked at the new arrival. He was *old*. The man had to be close to ninety. He had a head of thinning white disheveled hair and a four-day growth of beard. He reminded her of Bernie Sanders.

"Hasn't anyone been taking care of you?" she inquired.

Sam could hear her words, but couldn't respond. This coma shit was starting to wear thin. He heard tap water running, and in a few minutes the voice was back and scraping at his whiskers.

"That's better," he heard her say. He then felt a bristled hairbrush stroke his hair.

"You look ten years younger." Abby then turned away before she could see the corners of Sam's mouth begin to smile.

* * *

Kendra had access to art supplies and was currently applying paint to canvas. She only painted clowns, and her cell was decorated with several of these purported works of art. This creeped out the other inmates and quite a few of the turnkeys. She was in a particularly poor mood today following her latest laundry mishap. Snide remarks came her way from several inmates wearing stained jumpsuits. They still took some pride in their appearance. Anyway, painting always seemed to calm her down. Maybe when she got out of the joint she could make a living selling her art at swap meets or on eBay.

"Shitfuck," she exhaled as she took a tissue and dabbed at a streak of red paint that had dripped from the clown's nose and onto a flesh colored chin. More than one guard had told her that her works reminded them of those produced by John Wayne Gacy—the infamous serial killer who raped, tortured, and murdered more than 33 boys in the 1970s. She took it as a compliment although she had never seen a single one of his paintings.

Kendra threw the tissue to the floor and collapsed on her cot. She had to get out of this place. Thirteen more months in a cage seemed like an eternity. Her thoughts drifted to her father-in-law, Rick Potter. That poor bastard had at least 30 years to serve for killing his ex-wife: a life sentence for a man his age. She had no reason to doubt that he had stabbed Tara and couldn't care less that she was no longer walking this earth. The thing that really pissed her off was that Nate hadn't inherited any of his mother's sizeable fortune. Tara Potter-Conley-Finley-Goldblatt had been married four times and had amassed a tremendous amount of wealth. However, all she left her only child was a framed nude of the victim stepping into a bathtub. Nate had sold the hideous work of art to his friend Marshall for twenty bucks. She didn't want to think about what Marshall was using that picture for.

8
YOU'VE GOT TO BE KIDDING

It was raining when the trio of Paul, Madonna, and Seth pulled into the parking lot of the prison that housed their dad. The gray skies and steady downpour fit their mood. The transformation of weather from fair to miserable was as daunting as Clark Kent changing into Superman. One day would be hot as hell, the next chilly with showers.

They had made good time, arriving at COR precisely at 2:00 p.m., which only gave them a 30-minute window to visit inmate #739365. Following signs to the visitors' parking lot, their path was suddenly blocked by a large crossing gate that descended upon them with all of the politeness of an armed guard, catching Paul by surprise and prompting him to hit the brakes a little harder than necessary. The car skidded on the wet pavement, stopping inches before the barrier, perfectly placed alongside an automated parking ticket dispenser of the sort normally reserved for parking structures and shopping malls.

"What the hell is this?" Paul groused as he rolled down his window. "We have to pay to visit dad in the joint?"

"Doesn't surprise me one bit," answered Madonna. "Between taxes and parking fees, the Government is trying to take every last cent."

Seth had a different take on the subject. "Maybe the extra money helps the conditions inside. Perhaps better food or recreational upgrades."

"Or fattening the warden's pension plan," replied Paul. He snatched at the ticket and found a parking spot in the slippery Kings County lot.

They walked in the pouring rain along the eighteen-foot barbed wire fencing and noticed blue-shirted inmates milling about in the asphalt yard, indifferent to the inclement weather. Some were shooting hoops, others lifting weights, and still more standing in small groups discussing, well, God knows what.

Madonna grabbed Paul's hand and instinctively shifted a little closer towards him as if he could protect her from the caged criminals. A tower loomed above, and the barrel of a killing machine glinted in a stray ray of sunlight. They walked past the long rectangular buildings of gray and steel that seemed to blend in with the elements.

"I hate this place already," said Madonna more to herself than her companions. Paul and Seth nodded in agreement.

"We won't have much time," remarked Seth. "Visiting hours end in thirty minutes."

They followed a small crowd into the secured entrance and successfully passed through a metal detector. Seth was surprised at the number of children queuing up to enter, and felt guilty for leaving Noga behind.

"It's a good thing I didn't bring my gun," joked Paul. Madonna elbowed him in the stomach. "Don't even joke about that. A sense of humor isn't a job requirement at this place."

They were all dripping rainwater as they approached the main desk. Madonna's thin blouse clung to her body like a second skin, leaving little to the imagination. Paul's tee shirt revealed his muscular physique, and Seth's wet hair was frizzing up like a Brillo Pad. They looked like they were returning from a wild weekend at Woodstock. Manning the desk was an aging sentry, seemingly plucked from Central Casting, and sitting out the clock to be fully vested in the state's generous pension plan.

"What can I do for you folks?"

"We're here to see Rick Potter," said Seth.

The guard/receptionist name-tagged 'Crawford' asked, "Can I see your visitors application?"

"Our what?" inquired Paul.

"All visitors have to complete an application and have it approved before being allowed in."

"We didn't know about that. Can we fill one out now? We've been on the road for over three hours," argued Seth.

"I can give you a form, but you'll have to fax in a completed application for approval. Once it's approved, visiting hours are Saturday and Sunday from eight-thirty to two-thirty. Have a nice day." Crawford looked past the trio and called out, "Next."

"Can't you make an exception just this once?" asked Paul.

Crawford's eyes displayed his displeasure. "Are you trying to make trouble?"

"It appears so."

Madonna grabbed Paul's arm. "Let's just go."

Paul gave Crawford his dirtiest look and took two steps toward the door before turning back to the guard.

"Wait a minute." He reached into his shirt pocket and took out the parking ticket, turning to face Crawford.

"If you're sending us away then I want my money back." He waved the parking stub close to the guard's face.

"No refunds," quipped Crawford.

They stood glaring at each other for a few seconds before Seth slowly pulled his older brother away. "C'mon Paul."

The three of them trudged back to the car in a light drizzle, unaware that their father was busy editing a bar mitzvah video and wouldn't have been allowed visitors under any circumstances.

*   *   *

Detectives Macfarlane and Morgan's unmarked cop car pulled up to Rosey's Tavern for a late lunch. Dining at this particular establishment was easier during off-hours.

"I've heard this place is great," said Morgan, the towering, thin, birdlike junior partner, who was not the freshest fruit in the produce department. Having an uncle as police chief was the oldest form of job security, and everyone at the Devonshire Division knew that.

His weighty and mustachioed partner agreed. "I've heard the same thing. There was a nice article in *The Times* food section last week."

"You still read the newspaper?"

"Call me old school. This will be a nice change from all that Korean food we've been eating." Macfarlane was referring to the Otofu House, the restaurant where they had been spending an inordinate amount of time.

"Kimchee *is* starting to get old, but it's good for you, and you've got to admit the scenery is breathtaking." Morgan wasn't referencing the cheap paneling with Korean travel posters tacked on scratched walls, but the beautiful Asian women who tended to frequent the joint.

"I've noticed, but it's not worth the horrible gas you get after eating." Macfarlane had wanted to say that for the last three months.

"You never told me that."

"Laying off that shit will be better for both of us."

A high school hostess with fresh acne and tired feet showed them to a table in the center of the restaurant, but Macfarlane pointed to a booth by the window. There were just a handful of patrons at this late afternoon hour, and the girl had no problem giving them their table of choice. The cop liked to look out the window and have a full view of his surroundings; it was a practice he had picked up from the film *Goodfellas*.

The hostess handed each man a menu and reached for a sincere smile, but her heart wasn't in it.

Morgan picked at his nose and perused the menu. "They're known for their meatloaf. My Aunt Shirley makes killer meatloaf, and a BLT to die for. She should open her own restaurant in Toledo, even though she is 92 and cooks using a walker. Takes forever to eat."

Macfarlane had a tendency to tune out his partner and was doing just that. The heavy cop surveyed his surroundings with the keen eyes of a seasoned detective. He saw a lone, nicely dressed senior citizen with a thin build and perfectly coiffed salt-and-pepper hair seated at a nearby table, a briefcase on the floor beside him.

His eyes next turned towards the bar, where the bartender engaged in conversation with a thick, balding man holding a glass of clear liquid in his fist. Macfarlane judged that the man was no gentleman. Some people just have a look about them.

At a booth by the kitchen, two girls dressed in blue and white cheerleading uniforms were giggling and picking at French fries. Macfarlane briefly regarded them before shifting his eyes back to the bartender. Something about him looked familiar, but he couldn't place him.

Morgan had been droning on about something when he spotted the cheerleaders.

"Will you look at those two? How can their parents let them out of the house dressed like that?"

"I thought you enjoyed women in uniform."

"I do. Women, that is. These are girls. What do you think I am, a pedophile?"

Macfarlane didn't want to continue this particular line of conversation, and fortunately, a waitress arrived at their table as if on cue.

"Hi, my name is Caitlin, and I'll be your server. Can I get you something from the bar?"

"Hi Caitlin," said Morgan in his sexiest voice. "Water will be fine, we're on duty. Has anyone ever told you that you have a beautiful smile?"

Macfarlane rolled his eyes, having heard this line before. Morgan hadn't met a waitress yet that he didn't want to get to know better.

Caitlin casually waved a ringed left finger in front of him. "I'll give you a few minutes." She walked off to check on another table.

Macfarlane turned to his partner. "Why do you do that?" he asked.

"Do what?"

"Hit on every waitress that serves us. Didn't you see that rock on her finger before opening your mouth?"

"I guess I missed it. Not the first thing I look at."

"You're a detective. You should be more observant."

Morgan looked at his partner and nodded. He then opened the menu and started the daunting task of selecting his meal. The choices were endless. They were still reading the menu when Caitlin returned.

"Have you guys decided?"

Morgan put his hand on his chin before answering. "I'm torn between the stuffed cabbage and the meatloaf."

Macfarlane was getting impatient. "Make a decision already."

Morgan looked up at the waitress. "How's the stuffed cabbage today?"

"Same as every day."

"You talked me into it. Is it really as good as people say?"

"Even better."

"I like to try new things. Culinary sensations are a lot like sex. Variety is the spice of life." She turned her attention to the man sitting across from him.

"And for you?"

"I'd like a pastrami sandwich on white bread with mayo and a pickle, and a side of German potato salad."

Caitlin sighed. "All-righty, then." She proffered a smile and turned toward the kitchen. Both men watched her sway away.

"Now there's a woman I'd like to see dressed in a cheerleader's outfit," remarked Morgan. His partner tuned him out again. Morgan was getting harder to work with every day.

He heard an interior door open and saw an older woman with platinum blonde hair emerge from the kitchen. He had no trouble recognizing Rosey Kern. The pair had interviewed her while investigating the Tara Potter-Conley-Finley-Goldblatt murder case.

A moment later Morgan's eyes nodded in her direction.

"Hey, we know her. I wonder what she's doing here."

"I'm no Sherlock Holmes, but Rosey *is* her name, and this *is* Rosey's Tavern." He now realized why the bartender had looked so familiar. He pointed towards the bar.

"And that's the son of the murder victim."

A light went on in Morgan's head. "That's it: the Potter case. Kind of feel bad for the guy. His mom is murdered, his dad will spend the rest of his life in prison, and his wife's in the can for attempting to rob the deceased."

"That's life. Some are just better at it than others." Macfarlane waxed philosophical.

"Do you think she'll comp us? I'm running a little short and this place isn't exactly cheap."

"Let's leave that up to her." Macfarlane took a sip of water and watched as Rosey made her way to the table where the distinguished-looking gentleman was eating alone.

She sat down next to him. "You keep coming here, people will start to talk."

"What can I say? I love the food and the atmosphere. Plus, it's walking distance to the office."

Rosey's burly boyfriend Ollie sat at the bar chewing his gum, jealously watching her flirt with the distinguished looking gentleman.

9

STUFFED CABBAGE AND GIGGLING CHEERLEADERS

Rick Potter was in his groove. When he was editing, it was like a batter in the middle of a hitting streak. He had spent hours going through the boxes that chronicled the life of a cherubic little Jewish boy who was about to become a man. He dismissed many of the photos that were either out of focus or repetitive, but still had stacks of pictures that had made the first cut. The boxes were now sorted into somewhat chronological order. Next up was the laborious process of scanning the photos into the printer that the warden had procured for him.

Time passed quickly when he was immersed in a project—any project, even one as simple as this. His mind drifted to the warden's pretty assistant, Zoe. She had made an impression on the imprisoned film editor who hadn't tasted true love since Cheryl's death. Eighteen years was a long time to be loveless, and it was likely to extend much longer. He was angry with himself for thinking that she was Chinese. He should have known better and was pissed that he had made a poor first impression. He wondered if she was married and what life experiences had brought her to the same locked-in facility that he found himself in.

He forced himself to get Zoe out of his head and started the scanning process. His thoughts turned to his family. Had they forgotten about him? Why hadn't they come to see him? Did they believe he actually could commit murder? Rick had no way of knowing that Paul, Seth, and Madonna had tried to see him that very day, only to be turned away.

*   *   *

At Rosey's Tavern, the detectives were scarfing up the remnants of their meal.

"That may have been the best stuffed cabbage I've ever had," said Morgan, prior to issuing a loud burp.

The cheerleaders giggled like, well, schoolgirls.

"This might be better than my Aunt Shirley's. I think it's the quality of the meat, and the sauce *is* a bit tangier. Although, the last time I tasted Aunt Shirley's cabbage was about ten years ago."

His partner tuned him out again, turning his attention towards the bar. The powerfully built, balding man had not taken his eyes off Rosey, who was in deep conversation with her male customer. Macfarlane noticed the glare in the man's eyes, and the fierceness of his jaw jutting up and down like some kind of piston engine. His cop's *spidey* sense was kicking in. He watched as the man took a long swallow of the clear liquid and gracelessly slid off the barstool like a kid falling off his bike.

Morgan was now going on about a cherry cheesecake he once devoured in Norwalk and was oblivious to what was going on around him. Macfarlane's eyes remained fixed on Ollie as he staggered towards Teddy Williams' table on his unsteady legs.

"What's going on here?" Ollie demanded of the distinguished-looking gentleman.

Macfarlane detected an eastern European accent.

The corners of Rosey's lips tightened. "Ollie, this is Teddy. He's a regular. How about going back to the bar, okay"?

Ollie shot her a defiant scowl, a particular look on her boyfriend's kisser that Rosey knew all too well. The two of them had been together for a little over a year and got along fine, for the most part. The exception was when he drank too much, and he looked plenty sloshed right now.

"This is *my* girlfriend," Ollie slurred for all to hear.

The insurance agent was not in the best shape and hadn't been in an altercation since the fourth grade. He turned to Rosey, grasping for the right words. When none came, he stuck out a limp hand and sported the signature insurance salesman's smile that had made him successful.

"How do you do? Teddy Williams." Ollie looked at the hand, grabbed it and started to squeeze. Hard.

"Hey that hurts."

Ollie yanked his hand forward and swung with his left. The punch connected to a slacked jaw that sent the agent reeling backwards, causing him and a chair to crash to the floor. Rosey went to her customer and shielded him from further damage. Macfarlane shot out of his seat and ran to the group.

"That's enough. Detective Macfarlane, LAPD." He flashed a badge too quickly for anyone to decipher. All eyes focused on the cop.

"Are you alright?" He said to the man on the floor holding a hand to his jaw.

"I think so."

"I saw the whole thing," Macfarlane explained. "That was assault. Would you like to press charges?"

Teddy hesitated before answering. He looked at Rosey, who appeared to be shaking. She looked genuinely scared, her eyes pleading a silent 'no.'

"I don't think so."

The man slowly picked himself up with a little help from the detective.

"Lunch is on me," said Rosey, who was grateful that Teddy was not pursuing this any further.

Macfarlane turned to Ollie. "I've got my eye on you. Now cool off."

Ollie never stopped chewing, but slowly backed away and returned to the bar.

"What the fuck?" said Nate, who had never seen his mother-in-law's boyfriend so violent. Of course he hadn't been in his mother's living room when Ollie filleted her with an ice pick. That was just six months ago.

Ollie finished his drink in one last gulp, hopped off his stool, and stormed out of the tavern with Rosey following close behind him.

Macfarlane reached into his back pocket, pulled out a plastic wallet, found a business card, and handed it to Teddy.

"Here's my card. If he bothers you again, call me."

Teddy rubbed his jaw, which was starting to swell. "Thank you, Detective. I don't think that will be necessary." Nonetheless, he put the card into his vest pocket.

Teddy returned to his meal, but was too shaken to eat.

"What was that all about?" asked Morgan when his partner sat back down.

"Who knows? Maybe it was a lovers' quarrel or some kind of food dispute turned ugly. I really don't know."

"Shouldn't we take him in?" said Morgan, motioning his head towards the door where Ollie just exited.

"Do you really want to deal with all that paperwork?"

"Good point. I remember one time about six years ago. I was walking in a park when . . ."

Macfarlane had tuned him out again.

Outside the tavern Rosey found the courage to confront Ollie. She had worked too hard to have him, or anyone for that matter, threaten her livelihood. Having cops within earshot made it easier as well. "This is my place of business, and you cannot start fights in the middle of lunch."

Ollie fought the urge to smack her but never said a word as Rosey ranted on. He just turned his back to her and kept walking.

10
SAM STIRS

Abby was finishing up her shift at Chatsworth Care and decided to check on the new arrival one last time before calling it a night. Out of habit, she knocked on his open door before entering the room, where she found Sam in the same position as when she left him. His head was on a pillow, eyes at half-mast. He looked at peace and she hoped that he was. She sat next to him and stroked his thinning hair. "Don't give up, sir."

Sam heard the voice of a goddess and struggled to speak, his eyes just a barely perceptible slit. Abby leaned in closer and whispered, "Can you hear me?"

Sam could hear her, but couldn't form the words to reply to the pretty girl staring down at him.

"Can you blink if you can hear me?"

Sam strained with all he had left and managed the slightest hint of a blink.

"That's fucking awesome," she cried out. "Oh, sorry for the language."

Sam blinked two more times and Abby could swear that there was a hint of smile on his lips.

*   *   *

Kendra was bored of painting. She had plenty of free time on her hands, but maintained the same limited attention span she had had on the outside. She attached her latest creation to the wall above the toilet with Scotch Tape, and then put away her paints and brushes.

She lay down on her cot and closed her eyes even though she wasn't tired. There was a lot on her troubled mind. She thought about all those bastards who had conspired to put her in her current situation. If her father-in-law, Rick Potter, hadn't used his ex-wife as a pincushion, she would have never been in a position to steal the jewelry off the dead woman's body. This was all *his* fault.

Kendra had gone to Tara's upscale townhouse to confront her about Cheryl's murder and to get her to pony up for years of missed income. The truth was that Kendra hadn't worked much and her income would have been minimal. What she really wanted was to extract some semblance of revenge. It was just her fucking luck to find the woman already deceased.

Nate hadn't been much help. He bartended at his mother-in-law's tavern for close to minimum wage and hadn't saved a nickel in all those years she was behind bars.

She wasn't pleased with her mother, either. Rosey had changed dramatically during Kendra's time in the hoosegow, morphing from a dumpy, unkempt alcoholic to an attractive and successful restaurateur. Her son Bryan had turned out pretty good and was now married to that Goth girl that she had once considered a suspect in Cheryl's demise.

"Shitfuck."

A passing guard heard her. "What did you say to me?"

"I wasn't talking to you. I was just thinking out loud."

The guard was all too familiar with this inmate. "Thinking is a step in the right direction, but it'd be a good idea to *keep those* thoughts to yourself. Otherwise, you could find yourself in the hole."

Kendra had spent a lot of time in the hole—or '*shu*' as the prisoners called solitary confinement—and was not anxious for a return visit.

"Sorry."

"And why don't you try painting fruit or flowers. These clowns are just a little bit terrifying."

"Yes, sir," she replied to the female guard with close-cropped hair.

"Excuse me?"

"I'll give it a try, but don't expect miracles."

The guard stared at her for a moment before shaking her head and walking away. There was no hope for this particular caged Picasso of the clowns.

11

HEAT WAVE

It was dinnertime, and day had dissolved into night by the time Seth's Honda returned to the family abode. The trio was tired and frustrated at having driven some six hours round trip to see Pops, only to be denied entry. Paying the ten-dollar parking fee only added to their misery. It wasn't the cash, but the principle that mattered.

"I need a beer," proclaimed Paul.

"Only one?" asked Madonna.

"Probably a six pack."

"How is that different than any other day?" Seth asked.

"It isn't."

Noga met them at the door wearing her dancing tights. "*A gutn yeder eyner.*"

Seth smiled at his daughter and looked to Boonsri for a translation. "It means '*Hello everybody.*' When are you going to learn Yiddish so you can communicate with your daughter?"

"Normal children speak English."

"Your daughter is not normal; she's exceptional. Have you heard her speak Thai yet?"

Seth said that he hadn't and made his way to the fridge. He was pleasantly surprised to see a case of Bud light.

"I thought you'd need it," said Boonsri. "How'd it go?"

"It didn't." Seth passed beers to Paul and Madonna.

"Did you say hi to Grandpa for me?" asked Noga.

Seth put his beer down and picked up his tiny dancer. "We didn't get to see him."

"*Bupkis*," exclaimed Noga.

Seth set her down and watched as she pirouetted into the living room.

"What happened?" queried Boonsri.

"We needed to fill out some kind of form before they'd let us see him."

"Red-tape bullshit," added Paul.

Madonna asked if she could help in the kitchen, but Boonsri politely declined. The galley belonged to the Thai woman, and she didn't require any help.

Seth said, "I'll do some research and make sure we won't have the same problem next time."

Madonna suggested that they try again next weekend and leave a bit earlier in the day. They all agreed.

* * *

A few miles away, Ollie was standing across the street from the Teddy Williams Insurance Agency, seething. If those cops hadn't been sitting in that booth he would have inflicted some serious damage to that vest-wearing asshole. The guy obviously had a thing for his Rosey, and he would have no part of it. The man had to be taught a lesson and Ollie was the tutor to do it. He had followed his nemesis all the way to his office—just a five-minute stroll from the tavern.

It was a workplace that was hard to miss, given Williams' penchant for milking every last drop of his namesake's fame for his own aggrandizement. The slogan, '*Don't strike out for your family*,' was painted in white letters within the outline of a baseball diamond and was featured prominently on a placard that hung in front of the entrance.

The sight of it fueled Ollie's anger, and he scoffed at what he perceived as cheap exploitation of the baseball legend. He had learned baseball from Nate from the hours they spent together at the tavern's bar. Nate was a Yankees fan so obviously Ollie became a Red Sox fan. The rivalry between the two teams suited his combative nature. He had come to love the game and had great respect for the players that made it the National pastime.

Growing restless as the minutes ticked by, he had already worked his way through one pack of Russian chewing gum and was starting on a second. For the moment he had no real designs on Teddy, but just wanted to know a few more things about the guy, such as where he lived and whether or not he we was married. He didn't have to wait long.

The interior lights went dark and the dapper senior citizen exited the building. He locked the door and strolled to the adjacent parking lot where he started up a late model Lexus. Ollie returned to his car and waited.

When the Lexus pulled out, Ollie was behind him.

* * *

As spring training ended and the regular season began, all of California was suffering through an unbearable heat wave. Temperature records were being broken daily, even as the current Administration continued to deny climate change.

At CCWF, Kendra was perspiring as she placed dirty, sweat-stained institutional uniforms into an industrial dryer.

"Shitfuck." Kendra was making twenty-one cents an hour for all her hard work and was routinely annoyed. "Fuck this," she said before parking herself on a nearby stool.

Prison warder Juanita Torres saw her sitting down on the job and came over. "Problem, Potter?"

"It's hot as hell in here. How about some air conditioning or ventilation or something?"

"You may not have noticed, but you're in *prison*—not vacationing in St. Moritz. Maybe you should transfer to the kitchen."

"That would be even hotter," Kendra snapped back. "Besides, I can't even boil water. How about putting a pool in this joint. I could be a lifeguard."

"In your dreams. Now get back to work."

Kendra watched the screw walk away before getting up and leaving the laundry.

"I quit," she shouted before going back to her cell. Her co-workers gave her a hearty round of applause.

12

DENIED

Nurse Mallet finished her shift at Holy Cross Hospital and steered the four miles through moderate traffic to Chatsworth Care. She was curious to see if the old cop had made any progress. The thought of keeping him company for a while couldn't hurt either one of them. She figured they both could use some good old-fashioned karma.

Jen checked into the deserted lobby, scribbled her name in the log, and found her way to room 305E. Dinner was served from 4 until 5 p.m., and most patients were already in bed by seven.

The door was slightly ajar as she entered and made her way to the bed. A full moon was rising and silhouetted the lone occupant in the double room. A night-light over the bed that cast shadows on Sam's face reminded her of the film noir movies from the 1940s. Jen was relieved to see that the resident was freshly shaven and that his hair was neatly combed. Someone in this facility cared, and that gave her hope.

The timeworn detective reminded her of her Gramps who had passed away during the holidays. Gramps had gifted her his old Toyota when he realized that, for him, driving had become an adventure—a *dangerous* adventure.

Jen pulled a chair closer to the bed and gently stroked his hair. "How you doing, Sam? Have you missed me?"

Sam could hear her words and strained to answer. His lips quivered, but the only thing emanating from his mouth was a silent breath. She talked to him for close to an hour about a variety of subjects currently in the news. As she was getting ready to leave, the door to the room opened.

It was Abby. "Oh hi," she said. "I didn't know he had a visitor."

Jen introduced herself and told the young intern that she had cared for Sam at Holy Cross Hospital.

Abby grabbed a folding chair that had been positioned against a wall and brought it over.

"You're the one who shaved his whiskers and combed his hair, aren't you?" asked Jen.

"Guilty as charged. I'm no doctor, or nurse, yet, but I think he's coming around."

Her remark caught Jen by surprise. "What do you mean?"

"I asked him questions this afternoon and told him to blink if he understood me. He did."

It was dark in the room and Jen had not noticed any optical activity emanating from Sam's tired eyes. "What did the doctor say?"

"The doctor hasn't seen him yet, but I'll make sure he comes by tomorrow," Abby replied.

Jen reached over and turned on a lamp. Sam's peepers were open and his head was turned slightly in their direction. "Sam, can you hear me?"

Sam blinked once.

"Are you in any pain?"

This time he blinked twice.

She turned to Abby. "I think you're right! This is amazing." Jen hugged the intern like their team had just scored the winning goal in a soccer tournament. She turned back to the detective. "Sam, can you speak?"

Sam blinked once and struggled to talk.

"You can do it, I know you can," cheered Abby.

Sam tried again and this time a small whisper was released from his mouth. It sounded like '*beer*,' but it was a start.

"This is fantastic, Abby. Make sure a physician sees him in the morning."

Abby said that she would.

They stayed a few more minutes trying to communicate with their patient before turning off the light and going their separate ways.

*　*　*

Seth had followed prison procedures, filled out the visitor's application, and been given the green light to visit. On Saturday morning, he, Paul, and Madonna had gotten up early and were on the road by 9 a.m.

"Think he'll be surprised to see us?" asked Madonna.

"I think that's a safe bet," said Paul from behind the steering wheel.

Seth was spread out in the back seat, still tired from his late night bowling match. The younger Potter lived an active lifestyle. He worked full time at the rec center, played softball on Wednesdays, basketball on Thursdays, and trolled the bowling lanes on Fridays where he had a 200 average.

"Are we there yet?"

"Funny. Go back to sleep," scolded Madonna.

Paul stepped on the gas, hoping to make it to Corcoran by noon.

*　*　*

Rosey was in her kitchen cooking breakfast for her grandson, Jefferson, who waited patiently at the table. The seventeen-year-old had a voracious appetite that made his grandma happy.

"So what do you have planned for today?"

"Going to the beach with Abby. Supposed to be in the 90s today."

"No global warming my fat ass," stated Rosey.

Ollie crept into the room as quiet as a shadow and sat down next to Jeff. When Rosey turned around she was surprised to see him. "Jesus, when did you get here? You could have said hello, or let me know you're here."

Ollie remained mum as Rosey poured him a cup of Vietnamese coffee and returned to the stove.

The two had barely spoken since the altercation at the tavern. Rosey had occasionally seen that particularly ugly side of her boy-friend, and hoped to never see it again. She folded an omelet, added seasoned salt, and placed it on a plate alongside four strips of bacon and a generous helping of hash brown potatoes. She set the plate in front of her grandson.

"Excellent," said Jeff before devouring a forkful of the spicy egg dish.

Rosey smiled and turned her attention to Ollie. "Get you something?"

Ollie took his time answering. "No . . . Maybe you should stay home today."

"On Saturday? No way. Maybe you should stay away from the tavern today."

"So you can meet your new boyfriend?" Ollie stared at Rosey and then took out a fresh stick of gum.

"I'm not even going to dignify that with an answer."

Jeff looked at his grandma and then to Ollie. It didn't take a rocket scientist to see that there was tension between them. A knock at the door dissipated the conflict before it could escalate.

"That's probably Abby." Jeff took an oversized forkful of omelet and went to the door.

"Hey Jeff, what's shaking?" Abby waited for an answer, but Jeff's mouth was filled with egg, and as he started to reply his half-chewed meal spewed from his mouth.

"Gross." Abby started laughing. As Jeff joined her, more food slipped from his mouth to the floor. They walked to the kitchen. "Something smells wonderful."

Rosey gave her a hug and asked if she was hungry.

"If I lived with you, I'd weigh 200 pounds."

The words struck a chord with Rosey, who had at one time tipped the scales at a robust 312 pounds. Abby hadn't known her then, but felt like she had known her all of her life. The truth was that it was only a few months ago that she and her mother Mona had shown up looking for Jeff's older half-brother Bryan. Bryan hadn't seen Mona in years and had no clue that he had fathered a daughter. Bryan and Mona had had a brief whirlwind romance and had now been married for close to five months. Abby and Jeff had hit it off immediately, even though technically Jeff was Abby's uncle.

"I'm almost done," said Jeff as he scarfed up what remained on his plate.

"Try to swallow it this time," chided Abby.

Abby was dressed for the beach, wearing cut-off jeans and a navy bathing suit top.

Ollie sipped his coffee, chewed his gum, and looked a million miles away. Two brightly colored wrappers lay on the table like discarded pieces of trash.

Jeff gulped the last of his milk. "Thanks for breakfast, we gotta get going."

"Have fun and don't forget sunscreen," said Rosey.

With that, Jeff and Abby left the building and Rosey began to wash dishes.

Ollie watched her for a moment before leaving the room.

* * *

Paul made good time on the drive to Corcoran, arriving just shy of three hours. He seized a ticket from the familiar automated attendant and, after parking close to the entrance, turned to Seth in the backseat. "You do have the paperwork, don't you?"

"Yeah, I have it. But that's a question you should have asked before we left."

Seth had a point.

Paul, Madonna, and Seth repeated their previous steps, passed though security without issue, and handed the guard at the desk— alas, the same jerk from the previous week—the completed visitor's application. This time the trio was wet with perspiration instead of rain.

Crawford took his time looking over the paperwork, then picked up a list and studied it.

"Sorry. Rick Potter's in solitary. No visitors."

"You got to be shitting me," moaned Paul.

"I shit no one," countered Crawford.

Seth demanded to know why his father had been placed in solitary confinement. His dad was not the type to cause trouble. In fact, he didn't even belong in prison.

"Don't know and couldn't tell you if I did. Try again next week."

Madonna chimed in, "We've come a very long way to see him."

The guard looked at her like she was on the other end of a robo-call. "You're breaking my heart."

"Aren't you on the old side to be a receptionist?" she asked.

"I am not a receptionist, Honey. And you don't want to make me angry."

Seth changed the subject. "At least give us our parking money back. This is the second time we've come all the way here, paid for parking, and been turned away. That's twenty bucks plus another tankful of gas."

"Next." Crawford was not the talkative type and had visitors lined up behind these nuisances.

The trio trudged back to the car in defeat.

"This sucks," said Paul.

No one disagreed with him.

13
SLUSHIES AND CHEMISTRY

The sun's rays beat down on the dry Southern California landscape with blistering intensity. At the Devonshire Division Police Station the air conditioning had died a rattly death some twenty minutes earlier. Detectives Macfarlane and Morgan sat facing each other, finishing up vending machine lunches.

"You'd think they could at least bring in a couple of fans," groused Morgan as he wiped away the perspiration on his brow with a sweaty hand.

His partner nodded in agreement. "Budget cuts. They need the money to save our pensions. Or what's left of them."

Morgan used a long straw to slurp his extra-large slushy. "You know, I'm still thinking about the stuffed cabbage I got at that joint last week. I would say that was one of the top ten meals I've ever had."

"You say that all the time, whenever you like something."

"Well, this was some kind of special: A perfect blend of cabbage and seasoned ground beef with just a hint of Indian spices. And don't get me started on the tomato sauce. Adding ginger snaps is pure genius. We really need to go back there again."

"It was good," agreed Macfarlane. "And a lucky thing we were there, too. That beefy dude would have taken that fossil apart."

"Yeah. Hey, didn't he resemble that character actor, Peter Lorre?"

"Never heard of him."

"No kidding? Peter Lorre? The movie *M*? *The Maltese Falcon*? The face of noir?"

Macfarlane looked at his partner and shook his head. "You're full of useless information, did you know that?"

"You don't have to get sore at me . . . So, do you think it could get any hotter in this place? If I wanted a sauna, I'd go to the gym." Morgan didn't wait for an answer that he knew wouldn't be forthcoming. He slurped his slushy.

"This has got to be the best slushy I've had in years: in the top three at least. And I got to tell you, cherry is an underrated flavor . . ."

While Morgan had slushies on his mind, Macfarlane's thoughts turned back to the altercation at the tavern. He had an uneasy feeling that the violence he had witnessed was a frightening glimpse of things to come.

*   *   *

Once again, Rick Potter was unaware that his sons had attempted to visit him. He was stuck in the hole working away on Sonny Goldberg's bar mitzvah video. Sequestered and free of distractions, he could toil at a relatively quick pace. The selected photos had already been scanned and moved to the timeline. He added a few video clips to the sequence, as well. In its current state, his epic creation unspooled at an unbearable 28 minutes.

"Better to have all the material together and then start to whittle it down," he told himself.

This was the same procedure that Rick had followed during his film-editing career, although at that time, an assistant had performed the grunt work.

He removed his fingers from the keyboard and rubbed them together. The repetitive motions demanded of his profession were unavoidable. Carpel tunnel syndrome was a common malady among film editors, and many of his contemporaries had undergone surgery for relief.

He popped open a Coke from the small fridge and wrapped his fingers around the can. The cold soothed his hands and gave him temporary relief from the heat. In the old days, when Rick had been a professional editor, he had taken similar short breaks in the evening. He and his assistant would sip Scotch from a portable bar in the shape of an Old-World globe and discuss the particular episode and life in general. He now thought back to those days fondly.

He tossed the empty can in the trash bin, wiped his mouth with the back of his hand, and sat down to run his sequence. It was a chronological arrangement that summarized the life of Sonny Goldberg, the grandson of a proud prison warden.

Watching his first assembly was bittersweet for the innocent inmate. He remembered his own son Nate's bar mitzvah, and a similar video that he had produced for him. Those were some good times. Cheryl was beautiful and very much alive. Nate, Paul, and Seth had been inseparable and did everything together. Rick and Cheryl had survived the teenage years and were fortunate to still live with their kids when they became adults.

Their idyllic life ended the day Kendra and her son Bryan moved into their home. First, she alienated Nate from his friends. After that, she turned him against his brothers, Paul and Seth. Finally, she destroyed Nate's relationship with Rick and Cheryl. In between, Kendra shot feral cats in the backyard because they annoyed her. She also burned holes in the carpeting with her meth pipe, and slammed doors until they fell off the hinges. It wasn't long before Cheryl was dead and Kendra was sent to prison. Rick tried to shake those images from his mind.

He wondered again why Paul and Seth had not come to see him. He didn't expect anything from Nate. He was estranged from his oldest son, a situation that was depressing but unavoidable. However, he believed he had a good relationship with his other boys. They were probably ashamed of their old man and he couldn't blame them.

Enough melancholy; he had a job to do. He shook family thoughts from his mind and set to work.

The warden had requested a twenty-minute video, but Rick knew from experience that that would be too long. Ten minutes would be ideal, but he would show the warden a twelve-minute version and suggest cutting a couple of minutes more.

An iron gate slid open somewhere in the distance, and footsteps echoed down the long concrete corridor.

Rick stopped the sequence and waited for his guests to arrive.

The massive shadow of Guard Hinkle landed first, followed by the man himself. He carried a box that looked small in his muscled arms.

With him was Zoe, wearing an off-white pantsuit and a lavender colored silk blouse. In the dungeon-like lighting, she looked like an angel.

"Annyeonghaseyo." Rick greeted her in Korean.

"You remembered." Zoe was touched.

"How could I forget? Social visit? If I had known, I would have cleaned the place up and had snacks."

The hulking guard wasn't amused, but Zoe giggled and said, "We should have called first. I don't know what I was thinking."

The cell door swung open and Hinkle placed the box on the table.

Rick opened it and glanced at its contents, which consisted of dozens of additional photos of the bar mitzvah boy. "More material. That's just what I needed. This will save the video." He hid the sarcasm in his response.

"These are the most recent pictures," said Zoe. "The warden wants to be up-to-date."

"Spoken like a true co-producer."

Zoe smiled, but Hinkle's face was non-committal. Rick doubted the guard had any sense of humor. Maybe spending one's adult life supervising convicted criminals robbed you of that. In any event, Rick was grateful to have company, especially when it included someone as pretty as Zoe. Her smile lit up the cell like high beams on a truck.

"Can I offer either of you a can of Diet Coke?"

Hinkle snickered, but Zoe said that she'd love one. Rick took three steps to the fridge, pulled out a can, and popped it open. Their hands touched during the exchange.

"You wouldn't let a lady drink alone would you?" Her eyes danced.

"You're right. Where are my manners?" Rick grabbed another soda from the fridge, raised it in a toast.

"To the bar mitzvah boy . . . And new friends."

"I'll drink to that," added Zoe.

She clinked her can against Rick's and took a long sip. He watched as the liquid slid down her throat, reminding him of a soft drink commercial from years ago. He hadn't seen anything that sexy in quite a while.

She caught his gaze and held it. "Can I see what you've done so far? I've always been fascinated with filmmaking."

This was hardly filmmaking thought Rick, but he was proud of his work and was happy to show her.

"If it's alright with Hinkle here," he said, pointing to the imposing guard.

Zoe turned to Hinkle with pleading eyes.

The large guard nodded his consent.

"I've never seen a rough cut before," said Zoe.

Rick rolled his eyes before speaking. "We don't use the term 'rough cut.' Rough sounds like we've just thrown it together. We prefer first cut or editor's assembly."

"I didn't mean to offend you." Zoe sounded sincere, and Rick was angry with himself for schooling her on editor etiquette.

"Sorry, force of habit. Keep in mind that this is a work in progress and will probably be half as long as it is now."

He hit play and they watched the movie unfold. After about ten minutes, Hinkle announced that they had to leave.

"But we're just getting to the good part," deadpanned Rick.

"It's going to be wonderful," said Zoe.

Rick thought she was just being polite. "Still a long way to go. Right now, it's about twenty-eight minutes long. It will end up closer to ten. I'm going to need music to make this thing right. Can you ask the warden for a three or four song play list? Something sentimental. Oh, and if you can, get the soundtrack to *Peggy Sue Got Married*. That score will have everyone in tears."

Rick watched as Zoe made notes on a small pad as cell phones weren't permitted on the prison floor. Her onyx hair was as smooth as silk and her mysterious dark eyes were hard to read.

Rick continued, "I'll add in the new material, generate movement to each photograph, and dissolve between shots. That, losing about fifteen minutes, and the music will really help."

Zoe smiled. "I'll get right on it. It's too bad I can't watch you work. I find the whole process fascinating."

"I'd like the company."

"Well, it's like watching someone work a crossword puzzle to me," interjected Hinkle, who didn't have a creative bone in his huge body. Being a prison guard suited him.

"Let's go. This prisoner has work to do," he said with cold finality.

"Come back when you can," said Rick with a smile. "Gets a little lonely in here."

Zoe returned his smile and winked. "I have to bring your music."

With that, the mountain of a man and the petite vision of loveliness walked out of the cell. Rick listened until their footsteps faded away.

There was something about that woman.

14

SCHMEKEL, FARKAKTA

Abby and Jefferson were lying face up on wrinkled, oversized towels sprinkled with sand. Their plan to escape the oven-like heat was going to the beach. Unfortunately, their idea was shared with thousands of others looking for similar relief. Both had remnants of SPF 30 sunscreen lotion smeared on their faces for maximum protection.

"So much for escaping the inferno," said Jeff.

Abby agreed. "Maybe we should have gone ice skating or to a movie."

"Or we could just go in the water."

"And get wet! Are you insane?"

The pair watched as kids built sandcastles and seniors dipped their toes in the water like they had done in childhood when life was simpler. Abby said, "As hot as it is, I noticed a little chill in the air this morning. Everything okay at home?"

Jeff took a moment to answer.

"Grandma and Ollie are fighting. Not sure what it's about, but they've hardly spoken to each other all week."

"That guy scares me. What's his story?"

"You know as much about him as I do. He used to be a customer at the tavern and then he and Grandma started dating. He moved in not too long before you came to town. I've seen him sneaking around when he thinks no one is watching. Kind of creepy."

"And what's with that gum chewing? I don't think I've ever seen him without his mouth in motion."

"I don't know, but it kind of smells like dirty socks."

"Yuck."

Abby turned on her stomach and asked Jeff to apply lotion to her back. He was happy to oblige.

The conversation shifted to school and their upcoming senior prom. Thus far, three guys had asked Abby out, including the quarterback of the football team. Jefferson had no steady girlfriend, or interest in going. Besides, it would cost a small fortune and Jeff was always broke. Nate was not generous with an allowance, and Jeff needed to concentrate on his studies instead of working if he wanted to graduate.

Next, they discussed colleges. While Abby was researching Ivy League schools with an emphasis in medicine, Jeff just wanted to graduate and hadn't thought much beyond that.

One thing was certain; he didn't want to end up like his father. Bartending in your 40's for one's mother-in-law may sound exciting to some, but to him it was like being waterboarded by the C.I.A.

"So, do you ever talk with your mom?" Abby was curious. Having a mother serving time had to be hard on him.

"No."

Abby knew by the tone in his voice that she had crossed a line and immediately regretted it. She reached for a less provocative topic. "So, how about those Dodgers?"

*   *   *

The weary travelers returned to their Northridge home tired and pissed. In the past two weekends they had driven a total of 12 hours, the net result of which amounted to paying $20 to an ungrateful parking kiosk and jawing with a nasty sentry.

Boonsri greeted them at the door with beers in hand. "So, did everything go okay?"

Seth popped open his Budweiser. "The paperwork was correct, but dad was in solitary."

"What'd he do now?" asked Boonsri. Like Noga, it had taken her some time to appreciate Rick Potter. His home base was Shanghai and he'd come back to visit only a handful of times. She knew the man meant well, but he had made a poor impression on his most recent visit: the one that had gotten him into all this trouble.

Boonsri asked again, "What'd he do?"

"The bastards wouldn't tell us," said Paul.

"Can I help with dinner?" asked Madonna. She knew the answer to that question, but floated it anyway.

"No thanks, it's all done," said the queen of the kitchen. As a rule, Noga was the only one allowed to help. Why should things be any different now?

As if on cue, Noga walked into the kitchen.

"Did you see Grandpa? Is he coming home soon?" Seth bent down to look his six-year-old moppet in the eye. "We didn't get to see him, honey. He was very busy today."

"*Schmekel, farkakta!*" Of all the Old World Jewish expletives for the child to pick up, she sure chose some winners, and these were among the more debauched. Had Seth himself understood the language, he most certainly would have reprimanded the girl, but oblivious to the words' meaning, she went about her way unchecked.

* * *

Zoe opened the door to her condo and turned on a light. It had been a long and interesting day. The warden's secretary kicked off her shoes, set her purse on the dining room table and unscrewed a bottle of Pinot Noir that she had recently purchased from Trader Joe's. She poured herself a glass, took a seat by the window, and glanced down at the street from her fourth story perch.

People were walking the streets and living their lives. Corcoran was a prison community and most of its citizens had ties to the penitentiary. Yet few of them had any knowledge of the criminal justice system, much less what it would be like to be cooped up in an *8' x 10'* cell. Zoe, on the other hand, knew that world all too well.

It was never her plan to become a warden's assistant—a term she found to be far preferable to *'secretary.'* She doubted that any young girl dreamed of working in a prison. Like many teenaged girls, she had wanted to be an actress. Everyone told her she had the looks and, indeed, she had given it a fair shot. After completing junior college in Ontario, Canada, she had moved to Hollywood and found an agent right off the bat.

She had a comedic sense about her and there were not many Korean actresses that had that particular quality. Her slender 5'6" frame and good looks gave her another advantage. On her very first audition, a casting director had given it to her straight, not even making a pretense of trying to mince his words:

"I'll be brutally honest with you, dear. You're one of thousands that come to LA every year looking for stardom. The truth is you're going to have to put out to get ahead."

Then, as matter-of-factly as if it were part of any routine talent assessment, he continued: "Speaking of head . . ."

Upon which he unzipped his pants and pulled out his penis.

Zoe had heard stories about the casting couch, but assumed that they were mostly blown out of proportion, to excuse the pun.

She looked down at his member and said, "Ouch, that's too bad. I feel sorry for you." She thereupon departed his office—and the city of Los Angeles, eventually settling in Corcoran.

All this took place long before the Me Too movement effectively leveled the playing field for female actors. Zoe may not have ridden on its coattails, but was proud to have a story to tell about facing up to Hollywood's culture of sexual abuse long before it became fashionable to do so.

She moved in with a friend in Kings County and found a job at the prison, which was the largest employer in town. A few promotions later, and she landed her current position.

She sipped her wine and thought about Rick Potter. The man was older, but there was something about him that intrigued her. Perhaps it was his deep blue eyes that seemed to sparkle like city lights. He didn't act like the other inmates whose eyes never traveled north of her breasts. He had a skill that she admired, a gentle manner, and a sense of humor. He had been genuinely embarrassed thinking she was Chinese and had found that kind of adorable. She had checked his file and was shocked to learn that he had been convicted of murdering his ex-wife. Zoe took a sip of wine, and pondered this unexpected revelation. He didn't seem to fit the profile, and she was a good judge of character.

Some people are not what they seem. Still, one never knows . . .

15
THE I.B.S PLAN

Sam was making incremental progress every day and was anxious to get back on the case; or at least help it along. His transformation was nothing short of amazing. He was able to digest soft foods and speak in whispers, which was not easy considering that his parched throat felt dryer than the Sahara in the middle of summer. On this Sunday afternoon he was sitting up and watching an *ER* rerun when he had unexpected visitors.

Nurse Mallet had brought Doctor Doctorow with her to examine the old man.

After a brief examination the doctor took off his glasses and turned to the nurse.

"Extraordinary. This is the reason that I love medicine, Jen. Textbooks and experience taught me that this man would never recover. I was wrong."

"You think?" answered Sam.

Both physician and nurse chortled. Doctorow then turned serious. "Sam, I'll consult with the doctors here and keep a close eye on you. You're on the road back, but it will be difficult. You'll need physical therapy and may never be back to 100 per cent."

"How about 75?" Sam asked hopefully.

His audience tittered.

The doctor's phone buzzed from inside his coat pocket. He removed it with the grace of a surgeon and studied a text message. "Oops, got to go. Sam, keep doing what you're doing. Jen, I'll see you tomorrow."

The soles on his shoes squeaked as he left the room.

Jen took a seat next to her patient. "Are you comfortable?"

Sam attempted to respond but coughed up phlegm from somewhere deep inside his chest.

Jen smiled and helped Sam lie back. "Try and relax. Don't try to say too much."

Sam nodded his head in agreement, his strength waning. Instead, he raised his arm to half-mast and pointed to the closet.

"What is it?" asked Jen.

"Shiiii . . ." He wanted to say shirt, but didn't have the energy. Though he had little hope of ever seeing it again, he needed to know whether a certain brightly colored gum wrapper was still residing in an evidence bag tucked inside his shirt pocket.

"Shit? Do you need to go to the bathroom?"

The tired detective closed his eyes and drifted off to sleep.

* * *

Kendra and June were seated on a bench in the exercise yard watching the other inmates arm wrestle, run laps, and complain about life's unfairness. All of the convicts had that in common. This particular pair of prisoners had no interest in physical activity.

"Shitfuck," groused Kendra. "I just got to get out of here."

June thought for a moment before saying, "The odds just ain't so good. Unless . . ." her voice trailed off.

"Unless what?"

"Well, I heard the only way to leave this place is to get yourself checked into the infirmary. There's less security there. Don't ask me how to do it, 'cause I don't have a clue. But I have heard talk."

Kendra didn't think getting admitted to the prison infirmary would be difficult. She had a sensitive stomach that had been diagnosed as irritable bowel syndrome, or IBS. The problem was, what to do once she was admitted. There was only one way to find out.

* * *

Some 241 miles away in Northridge, California, a disturbed Russian national was sitting inside his SUV, parked outside the home of a dapper insurance agent. Ollie had spent the past few days tailing the man that he considered his romantic rival. The truth was that Teddy loved the tavern's food and location, and had no interest in its proprietor. But, of course, Ollie had no way of knowing that. Teddy had been married for 48 years to his high school sweetheart and had never gotten over her death. Cancer had not only taken the life of his true love, but had taken the soul of her survivor.

From staking out Teddy's house, Ollie knew that the senior citizen lived alone with his dog. He didn't know what breed it was, but the animal he called 'Junior' seemed slow and old, and didn't pose much of a threat.

He spat a wad of gum out the window and opened a fresh pack. He tossed the wrapper into the air, where it briefly stayed suspended like a miniature kite. Seconds later, the airborne object descended with a life all its own, fluttering like a butterfly before executing a perfect landing.

16
EVERYBODY'S A DIRECTOR

Zoe pulled a flash drive out of her computer and knocked on the adjoining door.

"Enter," spoke a God-like voice from behind the wall.

Zoe was wearing a short leather skirt that showed an abundance of leg: a wardrobe choice she had specially designated for the eyes of a certain film-editing inmate toiling away in solitary confinement.

"I finished downloading the music for the video."

"Excellent. Have Hinkle get it to Potter right away."

Goldberg dismissed her with a wave of his hand and shifted papers around his desk. Zoe lingered.

Goldberg looked up. "Is there anything else?"

"I'd like to go with him," she insisted. "I've always been interested in the film business and would like to see how he uses these songs. I could also tell you how it's coming along."

Goldberg considered her request. He was anxious to learn how the video was progressing and this would be a good way to find out. "Sure. You can go, but don't stay too long. He has a lot of work to do, and we're running short on time. He doesn't need any distractions, and you, Zoe, are a distraction. You owe me one."

Zoe ignored his remark, backed out of her boss's office and called for Hinkle. In less than a minute, the gaoler loomed in her doorway, larger than life.

The imposing man gave Zoe the willies. She knew there was a fine line between cops and crooks, and in her mind Hinkle could have fallen into either camp. She thought about the prisoner they were about to see. Rick Potter was the antitheses of Hinkle. Could he really be a cold-blooded killer?

Rick was isolated in his dungeon of a cutting room, focused on the 20-inch monitor with the intensity of a dentist performing a root canal. The cell reminded him of the closet-sized, windowless room in the basement of a studio that he had once been relegated to while on assignment for a producer in Atlanta.

The video was now down to fifteen minutes, and he had variously embellished every cut with motion effects, dissolves, and other catchy transitions. All he needed now to complete his masterpiece was music and a few more lifts—sections of edited footage that are removed in the interest of better pacing or flow.

He hoped that Zoe would be the person assigned to deliver the music. Her image clouded his thoughts in a way they hadn't been in years. It was a feeling that was both familiar and foreign, like an old dream, or a distant memory fighting to come to the surface.

Rick knew that they could have no future together. *He* had no future. He was bound to spend his remaining days in a cell with a tall Ponzi schemer named Stretch and a revolving door of assorted liars, thieves, and con men.

Above this, Zoe was attractive—more than attractive, in fact—and at least twenty years his junior. She'd never fall for an old geezer like him. But stranger things have happened. There were women out there that wrote to prisoners, and even married them.

He could at least console himself with the fact that he still had an imagination, and that prison could never take that away from him. With so much time alone, he often gave free rein to that imagination, especially when it came to romantic thoughts. There's nothing like imprisonment to create a void in this arena, and in Rick's fantasies, Zoe's proximity and good looks went a long way to filling it.

He also wondered if his incarcerated friends missed him. He would never be able to tell them the reason for his seclusion, but knew they'd be curious. Maybe he'd get a reputation as a badass when he returned.

He could practically taste that first promised sip of Scotch.

Zoe followed Hinkle to the elevator and along a labyrinth of hallways until they neared the makeshift cutting room. Rick Potter heard two sets of footsteps approaching which made his heart skip a beat.

The scent of a familiar perfume arrived a few seconds before she did. Zoe looked even better than he remembered.

"Welcome to the edit bay. My home away from home . . . Away from home."

Hinkle unlocked the steel door and Zoe sauntered in. The guard remained just outside the steel bars, his eyes carefully monitoring the pair.

"I come bearing music," said Zoe. She held a flash drive in her extended hand and Rick gently transferred it to his.

Their fingers touched during the exchange like in a Michelangelo work of art. Her hand was soft, and he didn't want to let go of it. That gentle touch was the most intimate contact he had been with a woman since his last Shanghai massage, some seven months ago.

Zoe felt slightly embarrassed before asking, "How's it coming along?"

"Well, I don't see another Emmy in my future, but I've cut the sequence in half. It's still long, but it's getting there."

"The warden is anxious to see it."

"I bet he is."

"Can I see what you've done?"

"You can see whatever you want, as long as it's okay with Lurch here."

Hinkle glowered at Rick, but didn't seem to object. Zoe walked behind the editor and looked over his shoulder.

He smelled her delicate scent. White Linen. It had been Cheryl's fragrance of choice.

Rick inserted the flash drive and watched as the music files downloaded to the desktop. He then ejected the drive and returned it to Zoe.

Their hands touched again. He felt a connection, like an electric current that raced through his hand and continued to all his extremities. He stared into Zoe's eyes, which appeared to be looking right through him.

Rick collected himself. "I'm going to make a new bin called music, and drag the cues into it. I have one track for sound now, so I'm going to add two additional tracks for music."

Zoe watched as Rick manipulated the keyboard with the dexterity of a court reporter.

He dragged the first song to the timeline and placed it at the beginning of the sequence. It was a tune by Pharrell Williams called '*Happy.*'

"I love this song," said the enthusiastic warden's assistant as she started singing along.

Rick had never heard the tune before, another reminder of their age difference. He had to admit that the song worked with the footage.

"I'll have to adjust each image to the beat of the music, but you can get an idea of how it's going to work." He positioned in two other songs and ended with the *Peggy Sue Got Married* score.

They watched the entire fifteen minute sequence as Sonny Goldberg's life unfolded before their eyes: an entire life in pictures.

Rick snuck a couple of looks in Zoe's direction, and she seemed genuinely engrossed in the video.

When it finished, Rick turned around to gauge the reaction of his audience of one.

Zoe said nothing, but her eyes gave away her emotions. "That was beautiful, and I don't even know the boy. Warden Goldberg will love this."

"When does he want to see it?"

"As soon as you have it ready. The Bar Mitzvah's in three days and the warden may want to give you notes."

Rick laughed. "Everybody's a director. I once worked on a network show and showed a scene to our casting director. She liked it, but suggested her fourteen-year-old son may have some thoughts on how to improve it. We have a saying in the editing business: to run it is to change it."

"I think it's perfect."

Rick wanted to tell her that he thought she was perfect, but couldn't get the words out. Instead he said, "Thanks, you're a good audience. Working on this has made me feel almost normal. It's good therapy."

"You appear well adjusted considering the circumstances. If you don't mind my saying, you seem different than the other inmates."

Rick's expression darkened and she instantly regretted her choice of words. "I mean men. I don't know you well, but it's like you don't belong here."

Rick was touched. "Thanks . . . I bet every man in here says he's innocent. But the truth is, I *don't* belong here. It's a long story, but I never killed anyone. I get queasy at the sight of blood."

Her expression softened, her eyes offering a window into her thoughts. She believed him. "I'll tell the warden that you'll have it ready tomorrow morning. Is that alright?"

"Perfect. Will you be coming, too?"

"I hope so." She tried to suppress a giggle.

The double entendre went right over Rick's head. He looked momentarily confused. Then it sunk in and he got her joke. "Don't make me laugh. People will think I'm having a good time."

* * *

Abby was exhausted and nauseous. She had cleaned out a dozen bedpans and was sick to her stomach. It made her have second thoughts about her current career path. She walked to the water fountain and took a good swallow. Her shift was officially over, but she wanted to check on Sam before leaving. He was improving daily and starting to speak in complete sentences.

Abby peered into his room and saw the old detective sleeping. She walked to his bedside and adjusted his blanket. She then started towards the door.

"Wait," said a voice that sounded every bit his age.

She turned around and saw Sam smiling.

Her face lit up like the morning sky. "I didn't want to wake you." She walked back to Sam's bedside. "This is so incredible. I knew you'd come out of it."

Sam returned her smile as best as he could. He raised a weak arm and pointed towards the closet. "My clothes."

"What about your clothes?" she retorted. "If you're thinking about high-tailing it out of here, you can forget it. You're too weak and— "

"Pocket."

Abby saw the serious look on his face and realized that whatever was in his pocket was important. She took a half dozen steps to the closet and removed his shirt and pants from metal hangers.

He waited anxiously as she walked toward him. He had lost all sense of time since he had collapsed on the cold pavement of a courthouse parking lot. He did know that he had come to this place from the hospital and at some point his clothes must have been washed. He raised a weak finger to the shirt pocket.

Abby reached in and turned his pocket inside out. Empty. The old man's heart sank. Abby could see the subtle change in Sam's features. He was clearly disappointed.

"Wait a minute," she told him as she returned to the closet. She bent down and picked up a large bag and brought it to the bed. "These are the rest of your belongings."

She reached in and brought out a wallet, wedding ring, socks, and underwear. Finally, she pulled out a plastic baggie with a rolled up scrap of blue paper inside.

"Are any of these things what you were looking for?"

Sam's eyes became moist. "Thank God."

He gripped her hand with renewed hope and strength—like a man half his age. Abby smiled and gave the old codger a hug. He held onto her like a drowning man clutching a ring buoy.

17
FRECKLES AND DIET COKE

Ollie was positioned behind the wheel, parked three houses north of Teddy Williams' residence. His mouth worked feverishly on a rubbery substance that had lost its flavor, but that retained its peculiar odor. A Russian folk song played on his upgraded factory-installed sound system.

Teddy hadn't been back to Rosey's Tavern since Ollie had confronted him, but rage still consumed the thickset man. Inside his twisted brain he believed that Teddy wanted to steal his girl away— something he would never allow to happen.

He had been a man of violence, but had kept those dark urges in check since gutting Tara with an ice pick. As a semi-retired member in good standing of the Russian mob, he knew how to deal with enemies, both real and imagined. He checked his timepiece, a classic Poljot Okean from the motherland. He knew Teddy's routine and that he would be coming home anytime now.

The stalker pulled out a fresh stick of gum, tossed it in his mouth and dropped the wrapper out the window.

* * *

Nate was in his familiar position behind the bar at Rosey's Tavern, chatting with his best friend, Marshall. Marshall was a low-level drug dealer and underachiever, who resembled the actor Johnny Depp. Marshall was popular with the ladies and had once slept with Nate's late mother: a fact that remained his secret. Tara had been a selfish lover and Marshall still felt guilty over their brief tryst. He was on his third rum and Coke, but the way his friend poured, it was more like his sixth.

"So, I meet this redhead at Jug-Jug and she was hot. We have a few drinks and I ask if she wants to smoke some weed at my place. She asked if I had any coke and I say, 'Yeah, sure.' She didn't need to know that I was referring to Caffeine-free Diet Coke. She then wants to know if she can bring her friend. I ask who is her friend and she points to a babe at a nearby table that's even hotter than she is. I say, 'Of course. Mi casa es tu casa.' It turns out that the friend is Swedish and doesn't speak a word of English. I love that. Anyway, they follow me home and get comfortable in the living room. I light up the bong and we start partying. Then they ask for the coke. I go to the fridge and pull out a couple cans of soda. I thought they'd be pissed, but they just started giggling. I'll tell you, these girls know how to party. I get them both in the hot tub; naked as the day they were born. The redhead has freckles all over her body, and I mean everywhere. The three of us go at it for hours. It's a wonder I can still walk."

Marshall enjoyed bragging about his sexual conquests, devoid of empathy for his friend whose wife was suffering behind bars in Central California.

"That's great, Marsh. I vaguely remember having sex. I hope you wore protection."

"And ruin the moment?"

Nate could only imagine what diseases could be swimming in his friend's body. He changed the subject. "Interesting thing happened here a while ago. Ollie attacked a guy on table seven."

"No shit?"

"If a couple of cops hadn't been here eating lunch, I think Ollie would have torn him apart."

"What did the guy do?"

"He was chatting with Rosey."

"Bastard."

"Ollie doesn't talk much, but I guess he has a temper."

"I'll remember that next time I engage your mother-in-law in conversation. So, as I was saying, the redhead's Swedish friend used to be a gymnast. She could have been a pretzel in a previous life."

Nate smiled and started washing a margarita glass as he listened to his friend's tales of debauchery.

* * *

Sam had come out of his coma, but still had a long road to recovery. Abby was by his side, taking notes on her iPhone 10.

"That's odd. It just occurred to me that I've seen this wrapper before. It has Russian lettering on it, right? It's all Ollie chews."

Sam raised an unkempt eyebrow.

"Take your time, and tell me what this is all about."

His voice was halting, but full of purpose. He painfully explained that he had discovered the unusual gum wrapper near the crime scene, and an identical one at the courthouse during Rick Potter's trial. The rareness of the paper could not have been a coincidence. Something was definitely wrong with this picture.

"Keep the wrapper in the bag. Fingerprints." Sam briefly closed his eyes before continuing. "Macfarlane. Devonshire Division. Bring him here. Please."

"I'll do my best."

Sam wanted to know more about Ollie. Abby explained that he lived with Rosey, was foreign, and gave her the heebie-jeebies. That he chewed his smelly gum like most people breathe air. Sam couldn't believe his good luck. This young intern knew the suspect.

Just then nurse Mallett appeared at the open doorway. "Hi, guys." She came into the room and pulled up a chair next to Abby. "How's our patient doing today?"

"You're not going to believe this."

As Abby filled Jen in on the clue in the closet, Sam closed his eyes and drifted off to sleep. He dreamt of an old case that had bothered him some thirty years ago.

Old cop dreams haunted him like Halloween spirits.

18

APPENDICITIS

It was dusk when Teddy Williams pulled up in his driveway and parked on asphalt in need of repair. He exited his car, looked around, and tripped on a sprinkler head. He got up, brushed at his grass-stained slacks, and then practically ran inside his house.

Ollie waited ten minutes before leaving the confines of his vehicle. Approaching Ted's front door, he heard classical music drifting from somewhere inside the house. He rang the bell and stepped out of view.

The music lowered, a dog barked, and footsteps approached.

Ollie heard a hesitant voice call out, "Who's there?"

Ollie didn't reply. The voice called out again repeating the same question: still no answer. Finally, he heard a lock turn and saw the door open just a crack. That was all it took for him to set his crude plan into motion.

For a husky man, Ollie moved quickly. He stuck a foot inside the narrow space between door and frame, and pushed his way through before Teddy even realized what was happening.

The door struck Teddy on the forehead, sending him sprawling backwards and crashing to the floor.

"Don't hurt me, please don't hurt me," Teddy pleaded. His voice cracked with fear as blood started dripping from the gash on his head.

Ollie pulled him up by the collar and looked directly into the taller man's nostrils as if they were a second pair of eyes.

"If you ever come near my Rosey again, I will kill you and feed your body parts to your dog."

Teddy couldn't quite grasp the full ramifications of the threat because he had trouble deciphering the powerful man's Russian accent. "Can you say that again? Please?"

The request only served to inflame Ollie further, and this leviathan of a man felt a sudden rush of adrenalin, a sensation he hadn't experienced since stabbing Tara. Rather than dignify his interloper with an answer, Ollie delivered a sharp punch to his throat. Teddy dropped to his grass-stained knees like a back-alley hooker and started to gag.

"I can't breathe," gasped Teddy before collapsing to the hardwood floor.

Ollie looked down at the figure struggling for breath and clutching his neck. He had used this punch often and found it effective.

Ollie spit out his gum. It landed in Teddy's hair, prompting the ex-mobster to chortle like a schoolyard bully. He had intended to send a message and had achieved his goal. Violence had been lurking just beneath the surface, and it felt good to let it out. He knew from experience that his injured adversary would be too frightened to go to the police.

* * *

The sky turned a pretty shade of violet as night replaced day. On the Potter deck, Paul, Madonna and Seth were making plans to visit their dad again.

"Let's try again this weekend," suggested Madonna. "We should have gone weeks ago."

"We did go weeks ago," said Paul. He turned towards his younger brother. "This time call and make sure that we have all the paperwork, *and* that he's out of the hole. I can't imagine what put him there."

"Maybe he complained about the food," joked Seth.

Just then, another mosquito saw the light and bit the dust. *Zzzzzzzzzzzz.*

Madonna slapped her arm. "Maybe we need two zappers out here," she quipped, shifting her attention from the fresh bite to the nagging itch on her ankle.

Seth, who was as oblivious to the bugs as to Madonna's complaints about them, punched in numbers on his cell phone, motioning the others to be quiet as he held it up to his ear. "Hi. I'd like to . . ."

It took him a moment to realize that he was speaking to a recording. Paul and Madonna watched as he pressed another digit. Then another. And another. He finally hung up.

"Why couldn't they tell me from the start I wouldn't be able to talk to a real person after five-o'clock?" he bellowed.

"Figures," groused Paul.

"I'll try again tomorrow," said Madonna, who continued scratching her ankle.

Boonsri appeared at the sliding glass door, interrupting their conversation and itching.

"Dinner's ready."

They were already on their feet before she could get the words out.

* * *

Abby wanted to be absolutely positive that the gum wrapper in Sam's baggie was identical to the brand that Ollie chewed. There was so much at stake that she started to doubt herself. This would require some expert sleuthing, so she decided to call Jefferson and invite herself over.

"I'm bored," she carped when he answered her call. "Maybe we can play some video games or something."

"That's exactly what I'm doing now. Come on by."

Abby jumped into her blue Hyundai feeling very much like Nancy Drew.

Jeff shared a guesthouse with Nate that was located directly behind Rosey and Ollie's main residence. It was a small but comfortable space, and rent was free. Nate worked all the time, so for the most part, Jeff had the place to himself.

It took just ten minutes via surface streets for Abby to arrive. She smiled at the toilet-shaped mailbox that greeted visitors and went through the side gate to Jeff's place. The door was open. "Don't you ever worry about mosquitos?" she asked upon entering.

"No. Should I?"

"They're driving us crazy." She had that in common with most people living in the San Fernando Valley. Abby closed the door behind her. "Maybe you should invest in a screen door."

On the 40-inch monitor that was the room's most prominent feature, Abby saw the frozen image of an animated soldier holding an AK-47 and four enemy combatants lying in pools of blood. She pointed to the screen, "Lovely."

"Want to play?"

"Not that game. To be honest, I'm kind of hungry. You think Grandma's got anything good to eat?"

"Are you kidding me?"

She followed Jeff out the door and into the main house. A light was on in the living room, but all was quiet. "Where is everyone?"

"Beats me. Probably at the tavern," said Jeff, who inserted his head into the open refrigerator while Abby surveyed the kitchen. The counters were spotless and the table empty. "Looks like fried chicken or meatloaf," came a muffled voice from inside the fridge.

"Meatloaf sounds great."

Abby cast her eyes to the trash can in the corner. It was filled with paper towels and other assorted kitchen garbage. If a wrapper were to be found, this would be the place.

Jeff reached into an overhead cabinet and pulled out a couple of plates. He cut two healthy slices of the meat dish and placed them in the microwave, setting the timer for 90 seconds. He then went to a drawer by the sink for cutlery.

"That smells so good," commented Abby.

There wasn't anybody who didn't love Rosey's cooking. Jeff pulled a couple of sheets off the electronic paper towel roll and waited for the appliance to ding. "So, how's the job?" he asked.

"I love it, well most of it. Not a big bed pan fan."

"Sounds disgusting. I couldn't do it."

"You could if you had to, but *you* don't have to. You know a part time job wouldn't kill you."

The microwave chimed just in time: saved by the bell. Her argument echoed that of his father, who was always getting on him about finding a job—something Jeff was not interested in exploring at this stage of his life.

He removed the dish from the microwave and put a portion of meatloaf on each plate. They sat at the kitchen table digging into the Tavern's signature delicacy.

"This is wonderful," remarked Abby.

"That's why her restaurant is so successful."

Abby and Jeff were close and could talk about anything, but she was reluctant to include him in her quest for the wrapper. How could she properly explain her mission? That she was on some kind of weird scavenger hunt? What If Ollie had nothing to do with Tara's murder? At this point in her mini-investigation, it would be better not to involve Jeff. She took another forkful of meat from her plate. She needed to get back to the task at hand and dig into that trash. "You wouldn't happen to have any wine, would you?"

"My dad has a couple of bottles out back. Red or white?"

"A merlot would pair perfectly with the meatloaf."

Jeff smiled and headed out the back door to fetch the vino. The moment he was out of sight, Abby wasted no time rummaging through the garbage. Banana peels, coffee grounds, and plastic bags abounded. "Yuck." She felt like she was back at work dealing with human waste. She then spotted the unmistakable shade of the wrapper she was seeking and, plucking it free from coffee grains and bits of orange peel, carefully held it by the edges and stuck it in her pants pocket. She started putting the trash back.

"What are you doing?" asked a voice with an unmistakable Russian accent.

Abby jumped about two feet in the air. "Jesus Christ, you scared the shit out of me!"

"You haven't answered my question."

Abby had to think fast. "The trash was knocked over and I was just cleaning up the mess," she stammered.

Just then, Jeff came into the room holding a bottle of red wine in the air like a trophy. He stopped when he saw Ollie.

"Oh shit. We were just getting a snack."

Ollie eyed Abby suspiciously. Something wasn't right, but he didn't know what. He turned and walked into the den.

Abby leaned over to Jeff. "He scares me," she said in an unsettled whisper.

"Tell me about it. He's like something out of a Stephen King novel."

They decided not to open the wine; after all, they *were* underaged. Wary about saying anything that might incite their interloper, they engaged in small talk while finishing their meal.

Abby was too unsettled to relax. "I think I should go."

Jeff looked at her, surprised. "You just got here."

"I know, but I'm kind of tired and have a busy day tomorrow. I go to school *and* work. You should try it."

They hugged each other and said they'd meet up next week. Abby power-walked to her car with the gum wrapper tucked neatly inside her pocket.

As she pulled away from the curb she was sure that Ollie was watching her.

*   *   *

"Shitfuck," screamed Kendra at the top of her lungs. She doubled over in apparent pain.

Two guards rushed to her cell. "What the fuck is your problem?" asked the taller of the two women.

Kendra just groaned in response.

"Looks sick," added the more diminutive guard.

"Ya think?" asked her sarcastic partner.

"Help me, I am sick, goddammit." Kendra continued to whimper while clutching her stomach. She wasn't much of an actress, but the guards weren't exactly theater critics, either. "Better take her to the infirmary. C'mon, grab her arm."

The pair of guards, whom inmates called 'The Two Stooges' behind their backs, each took a side and walked their patient to the sickbay.

Kendra had no escape plan. Yet. But she did want to get the lay of the land, and check out what had been described to her as the best chance to leave this place on her own terms.

*   *   *

Rick was a morning person and woke up around 6:30 every day, give or take a few minutes. He went to the small fridge in the corner of his cell and pulled out a Danish. It was almost like visiting craft services on a movie set.

He wanted one last view of the video before the warden's 9:00 a.m. screening. He anticipated that the warden would give him notes. When it came to the finalization of a movie, everyone gave vent to their opinions, whether they be positive, negative, or indifferent. That was part of the process.

Rick hoped the Warden would bring Zoe with him.

He couldn't get her off his mind.

* * *

Kendra was hoarse from all of her phony groaning while an older man with a reddish nose, a receding hairline, and bifocal glasses applied pressure on her abdomen. Researching a plan for escape had its consequences.

"This is bad. Real bad," said the diagnostician, who may or may not have had a medical degree.

Kendra's head shot up. "I'm feeling much better. Really."

"Young lady, you have appendicitis," declared the medical practitioner, who was evidently a doctor, after all. "We're going to need to operate."

"Shitfuck!" she gasped.

"Nurse, prep for surgery."

A middle-aged nurse shaking with the onset of palsy brought a surgical gown for Kendra to change into.

"Put this on," she said with all the affection of the Wicked Witch of the West. She started to unzip Kendra's jumpsuit.

"Get your hands off of me, you . . ." a searing pain stopped Kendra from continuing. "Someone help me!" she screamed.

"I would if you'd let me," said the nurse as she undressed the reluctant patient and helped her into the gown.

The prison had a small but adequate operating room for emergencies such as this.

"I'm feeling better now." Kendra protested. She tried to slide off the exam table, but to her astonishment, suddenly doubled over in pain. Could something much worse than her IBS suddenly have overtaken her digestive system? It was hard to believe, but the evidence was all too convincing: she *had* ruptured her appendix. That would be just her fucking luck.

The nurse stuck a needle into her arm and within ten seconds she was out.

19

SCREENPLAYS AND RESTRAINING ORDERS

Warden Goldberg woke up early and devoured a hearty breakfast of scrambled eggs, bacon, hashed brown potatoes, and a side of toast lathered with orange marmalade. His wife was a former short order cook and her dishes were almost as good as the food served at the tavern. One particularly large glob of marmalade had somehow missed his mouth, leaving an orange stain on his checkered sports coat.

"Now look what you've done," scolded Mrs. Goldberg. "I can't take you anywhere."

She dabbed at the stain with tap water, which widened the blemish into a shape that vaguely resembled the nation of Wales.

"It'll dry, and no one will notice. Today's the big day. I'll get a look at Sonny's video."

"It was nice of that man to do this for us," said Mrs. Goldberg.

"It wasn't like he had a choice." The warden kissed his wife good-bye and headed into the office.

At precisely 8:55 a.m., Guard Hinkle arrived to escort the warden to the makeshift cutting room. He glanced at Zoe, who was wearing a short black skirt and a scoop-necked mauve blouse—attire more suited for a night on the town than work in a penal office.

"Going out tonight?"

Zoe thought fast. "Ah . . . No . . . Laundry is piling up. This is the only clean outfit I have left." She tapped a digit on her phone and the warden appeared like magic. "Morning, Warden," said Zoe.

Hinkle pointed to a large spot on the Warden's coat. "You have a little stain right there."

Goldberg glared at him. "When I want your opinion on my wardrobe, I'll ask for it."

Zoe found an opening to ask, "Can I come, too? I'd really like to see the video."

Goldberg rarely turned down small requests from his comely assistant. She looked like expensive champagne and smelled like honeysuckles, and today was no exception.

"Sure, you can come, but you—"

"Owe you one. I know."

The trio arrived at Rick's cell/editing suite a few minutes later. Rick turned from some last-minute color-correcting in order to greet them.

He looked directly at Zoe. "Annyeonghaseyo."

The warden gave the editor a blank look while Zoe slyly smiled and returned his greeting. "Annyeonghaseyo."

Rick turned his attention to the warden. "Who's minding the store?"

"What's our length?" Goldberg responded, getting down to the business at hand.

"Spoken like a true producer. Twelve minutes and thirty-five seconds."

"I wanted it longer," declaimed the warden, the force of his authority showing itself.

"I can always pad it, but it works really well at this length. Trust me."

"Trust you? You're a convicted murderer—"

"With an Emmy Award in editing," said Rick, completing the warden's sentence.

Zoe winced and Hinkle chuckled from outside the cell.

The warden clearly was not amused as he and Zoe pulled up chairs on either side of the editor.

Rick's eyes were momentarily riveted by Zoe's appearance as she seated herself, and he gave her his best smile. "Wow," he let out softly, unwilling to risk saying more.

"I'm excited to see this," she responded, exercising some restraint of her own.

He was excited to see *her*, but couldn't tell her in front of the others.

"Roll 'em," commanded the warden, again sounding like a producer or studio head.

Rick pecked at the keyboard and the sequence sprang to life.

For the next twelve minutes and thirty five seconds, Zoe oohed and aahed while Goldberg discreetly wiped away a tear with a magician's sleight of hand. His grandson Sonny would be a man in a couple of days, and this film would be a testament of his entire life up to this point—or a condensed version of it, at least.

When the music swelled and the picture faded out, Rick stopped the computer and waited for comments. It had been a long time since he had been in such a position, but the feeling of anticipation came back to him with the immediacy of knowing how to ride a bike. How many times in his life had a director or producer stood behind him waiting to criticize his work?

Zoe spoke first in a halting voice. "I think that was just beautiful."

Rick appreciated her positive review. In his experience, the first comment usually set the tone for the other viewers.

"I think it could be a little longer," said Goldberg. "But maybe you're right. You've done a very good job. You sir, have earned your Scotch."

"Thank you. And you've got a fine grandson, Warden."

Goldberg stood up with an approximation of a grin on his face. "Maybe I can post this on YouTube, see how many hits it gets. Zoe, look into that for me." To Rick he said, "I'm going to need a dozen copies for family."

Rick thought for a moment and said, "In that case I'll need an external DVD drive, and software called Roxio Toast Titanium. Oh, and a dozen Blue Ray discs." He took a closer look at the warden's jacket and pointed. "Did you know you have a stain right there?"

Hinkle chuckled. The warden ignored Rick's observation and turned to his assistant. "Zoe, take care of it ASAP."

"Yes, sir. Right away."

The warden took two steps toward the door, stopped, and turned toward his editor. "One more thing. I have this screenplay that I'd like you to read. It's a drama that I wrote in college, but I think it holds up."

From outside the cell Hinkle coughed to suppress his amusement.

"Sure, I'll try to fit it into my busy schedule," Rick said wryly. "I'll give you my honest opinion. But surely there must be some real writers in this joint?"

"We have several, but they're either romance novelists or prolific wordsmiths of pornography."

"Sorry I asked."

Goldberg said, "Then we're done here," and began to walk off. Zoe winked at Rick and then followed her boss out of the cell like a baby duckling. The editor's heart fluttered like a butterfly.

* * *

Jennifer Mallett picked up Abby after her shift at the hospital. They planned to go to the Devonshire Station together and seek out Detective Macfarlane. Sam Beetley was literally staying alive until the gum wrapper clues were investigated.

"I did some research last night," said the high school honor student. "It's not sold in the States. Has to be imported from Russia."

"I bet there's not too many ex-pats in the States that would go to that much trouble for a stick of gum," Jen theorized.

And on the face of things, she was right. Who would go to such lengths to import chewing gum? It's not like it was some highly sought-after Vodka: the character and flavor of which could only come from Russia.

"My gram's boyfriend chews it. Stinks something awful."

"The boyfriend or the gum?"

"The gum, but he's not as fresh as a daisy either."

They both laughed as Jen turned south on Reseda Boulevard and headed towards the police station.

*   *   *

Teddy Williams was a wreck. He paced the living room in circles, with Junior watching his master's every eccentric move with curious amusement. Teddy had locked each door and window and still didn't feel safe in his own house. That maniac in the tavern had followed him home and savagely attacked him. Now, he had a headache and a knot on his forehead the size of China. Swallowing was difficult, courtesy of a fist to his throat.

He made a mental note to go to Costco and buy a home security system. One thing was for sure: he was never going back to that tavern again—the taste of the food be damned.

Teddy was not a drinker, but took an occasional pill when he felt stressed. And now he felt stressed. He marched to his bedroom and reached for the pillbox on his desk.

The prescription Lexapro was in a childproof container that took the nervous man a few minutes to open. He popped two into his mouth and rested his arms on the desk.

He glanced down and noticed the business card that the detective had given him during the altercation at the tavern. He remembered the hefty cop telling him to call if he needed him. Well, he needed him, all right.

Fuck the telephone, he thought. Teddy reached for his car keys. He needed to file a restraining order against that fiend as soon as possible. In fact, right now.

Teddy patted his pet, put on a Cardigan sweater, and carefully snuck out the back door.

20
TED WILLIAMS STRIKES OUT

Kendra was groggy after awakening from a 70 minute operation to remove her ruptured appendix. How many aspiring prison escapees in history have had just the fucking luck to enter the infirmary on a scouting mission for a bust-out, only to have an ill-timed medical emergency? She was convinced she had to have been the first.

"Shitfuck," she moaned to an empty room. She was hooked up to an IV and lying on a cot outside the operating room. There would be no escapes for her in the near future.

She attempted to look around the small in-house hospital, but got dizzy and passed out.

*   *   *

Detectives Macfarlane and Morgan were at their desks catching up on paperwork due a week ago.

"So, how about those Dodgers?" chirped Morgan.

It was close to quitting time after a long and humid day and Macfarlane was in no mood for small talk. He wanted to go home to his humble abode and fry up a steak with an expiration date that had expired two days ago.

"Too early to tell, but they've been good for over 30 years without winning another World Series." He instantly regretted saying something that would get his partner worked up. Once Morgan started to rant, it was almost impossible to stop him.

"It's not the team's fault. I blame it on their manager, Dave Roberts." Macfarlane turned away, but Morgan continued anyway. "The guy just doesn't know how to use his bullpen. And don't get me started on his platooning."

"How about we call it a day. I'm beat," yawned Macfarlane.

Morgan was about to agree with his partner when the landline telephone rang. Macfarlane regarded it with mild irritation and then reached for it. "Why do calls always have to come in when you're ready to go home?" he grumbled, half to himself.

"Macfarlane," he barked into the decades-old receiver. "Who . . . I see." He put his hand over the mouthpiece and explained to his partner that there were two women here to see them on an important matter.

Morgan shrugged his shoulders.

"Okay, send them in."

Jen and Abby were escorted into the detective bullpen (not to be confused with the Dodgers' bullpen), and led to the two weary constables. Macfarlane stood up, while Morgan remained seated.

"What can we do for you?" Macfarlane asked, motioning for them to take a seat.

The elder woman spoke up. "I'm Jen and this is Abby. I'm a nurse at Holy Cross Hospital and Abby's an aide at the Chatsworth Care Rehabilitation Center."

Morgan studied the two visitors. One looked young, but not illegal. He judged her to be at least eighteen. She had full lips and russet-colored hair that cascaded down her shoulders. She looked like an athlete and wore her pants tight. The second lady, Nurse Jen, looked about ten years older. Her piercing blue eyes caught Morgan staring at her and he abruptly turned away.

Jen resumed her role as spokesperson. "There is a patient at the rehabilitation center that asked us to contact you. He's a retired detective named Samuel Beetley."

"Who?" asked Morgan, who turned toward his senior partner.

"Beetley. I remember him," said Macfarlane. "A good cop, before your time. Saw him last year nosing around." He looked at the two women. "How is he?"

"Getting better," offered Abby, who then looked toward Jen to continue.

"He was in a coma, but came out of it. He's still weak, but insisted we see you. Something about a case you worked on. He's not able to get out of bed, but needs for you to see him as soon as possible."

*　*　*

Teddy Williams pulled into the Devonshire Division parking lot and looked to see if he had been followed. He assumed he was safe in a police parking lot, but the maniac had attacked him in a public place before. Was anyone really safe anywhere?

He pushed open the glass door and approached the desk sergeant on duty, showing him Detective Macfarlane's business card and asking to see him.

"It's a matter of life and death . . . Mine," asserted Teddy.

"Have a seat." Sergeant Perez studied the agitated man before him. Life *and death?* He doubted that. The guy looked like a semi-retired accountant at the end of a grueling tax season. However, he did have a noticeable lump on his forehead and a bruised adam's apple.

"The detective is busy right now, but I'll let him know you're here. And you are?"

The insurance agent took a deep breath. "Teddy Williams. The victim from Rosey's Tavern."

"Ted Williams?" Perez snickered. "You used to be one hell of a hitter." Perez laughed out loud, causing his coworkers to look his way.

Teddy had been the butt of baseball jokes his entire life and was not amused.

"Haven't heard *that* one before."

Perez took a long look at the man before him. He was nicely dressed, but looked like he had gone a couple of rounds with Manny Pacquiao." Have a seat Mr. Williams. I'll let you know as soon as he's available. Can I get you a water?"

"No, thank you."

Teddy sat down on a splintered bench. He winced as a sliver of wood penetrated his rear end. Perez watched the man's legs go up and down, an affliction known as '*restless leg syndrome*.'

* * *

Back in the bullpen, Macfarlane eyed Jen. "So, you're telling us that Beetley found a gum wrapper and wants us to investigate?"

"Maybe it looked suspicious," joked Morgan.

"He says it's a clue in a murder case you investigated last year." Abby added, "The Rick Potter case."

"That was a slam dunk," said Macfarlane. "Potter admitted being at his ex-wife's place on the night she was killed, and his fingerprints were found on the murder weapon. He had motive and opportunity."

"Sam told us not to take no for an answer," pleaded Jen. "Would it hurt to just talk to him? You know, one cop to another." The two detectives looked at each other before she gave them her sweetest smile and said, "Please?"

Abby added, "Pretty please?"

Morgan's eyes softened. "Will either of you be there if we come by in the morning?" His partner threw him a look.

"I have school," said Abby.

"College?"

"Next semester. I'm going to be a nurse like Jen. At least I hope so."

Morgan had to suppress his contentment. At least she could be eighteen, after all.

"I can be there," stated Jen.

They agreed to meet at Chatsworth Care at 10:00 the next morning. Jen gave them directions and a smile. "Thank you so much."

After the two ladies left the room, Macfarlane relented. "I guess it wouldn't hurt to talk to the guy."

"Which one of them did you find more attractive? I know Abby is young, but she carries herself older."

"Is that all you think about? You're almost forty years old, for God sake."

"I'm in the prime of life, and a healthy heterosexual male. You should read "GQ." May to December romances are back in style."

"Let's call it a night, okay?" Macfarlane shook his head, turned to leave. "Good night, Randolph."

Ted was picking splinters from his slacks when he saw a pair of young women walk past him and out the door. He checked his watch and asked Perez, "When can I see the detective?"

The desk sergeant had forgotten all about the battered senior citizen. He picked up the phone and rang up the detectives.

Morgan grimaced at the sound of another call. "Should I pick up?"

Macfarlane was standing and putting on his windbreaker. "Protect and serve, remember? It might be important."

"So, that's a yes?" asked Morgan.

"Affirmative." Macfarlane sat back down as Morgan picked up the receiver.

"Morgan." He listened for a beat and said, "Jeez, we were supposed to be out of here half an hour ago."

"Want me to get rid of him?" asked the voice on the other end.

Morgan considered it. "Nah, send him back, but that's it for tonight."

Thirty seconds later Teddy Williams breezed into the bullpen. Recognizing the detectives, he went straight to them. "That brute came to my house and beat me like a drum. Look." He pointed to his head. "He could have killed me."

"Have a seat, Mister . . ."

"Williams. Teddy Williams."

Morgan burst out laughing. "I thought you died years ago. Froze your head or something."

"What can we do for you," asked the more sober Macfarlane.

"I'm afraid for my life. This guy is a stone-cold killer. I saw it in his eyes. I want you to arrest him, before he kills me."

"We can't just arrest him. First you'll have to file a complaint."

"What about a restraining order?"

"I can give you the form to fill out." Macfarlane opened a drawer, found what he was looking for, and handed an official-looking document to Ted. "Bring it back tomorrow."

Williams looked over the form. "How can I fill this out? I don't know his name or address."

"That's going to be a problem," said Macfarlane stating the obvious. "Perhaps if you went to the tavern and asked the owner."

"I'm never going back there again. I don't care how good the meatloaf is."

Morgan loved talking food. "Is it really that good? I had the stuffed cabbage and thought it was amazing, but now I'm thinking that I should have ordered the meatloaf. What, in your opinion, is the better entree?"

Teddy was still traumatized by the attack and didn't really want to get into a culinary discussion. "I don't know. Cabbage gives me gas." He looked to Macfarlane for help. "What should I do?"

"Well, I'd keep a low profile and be careful." Macfarlane didn't know what else to say.

Williams nodded and scurried out of the office.

Watching him go, Morgan mused, "Imagine going through life with a name like Ted Williams. My dad said he was the greatest hitter he ever saw. Of course he never saw Ty Cobb or Pete Reiser."

Macfarlane had already tuned him out and was heading for the door.

21

SCOTCH AND STATE-ISSUED COUGH DROPS

Rick Potter finished making the last of the DVD copies of the epic bar mitzvah video and got word to the warden that his project was completed. About an hour later he heard the sound of sliding steel gates and smelled the fragrant aroma of White Linen perfume.

His spirits brightened at the thought of seeing Zoe again. Rick smoothed his hair and tucked in his shirt in anticipation. And then she and Hinkle were at his cell.

"Hi. I was hoping you'd come by," announced Rick.

"Of course. I am the associate producer after all. How are you?"

"Better now." Rick couldn't take his eyes off her. She had her dark hair tied in a ponytail and looked almost girlish. Her perfume smelled like a spring morning after a rain and reminded him of Cheryl. His mind began to wander. He felt like he had when he was a kid and watched Annette Funicello frolicking on the sand in one of those bad beach movies.

"Are you alright?" asked Zoe. "You look lost."

Rick came back to earth. "Sorry. I guess I was lost . . . In thought." He handed Zoe the discs, who in turn passed them on to Hinkle.

She turned back to face the man she now regarded as an anomaly: an inmate with specialized talent and sophisticated tastes. "I have a surprise for you."

Rick's eyes grew large as she reached into a shopping bag and pulled out a silver flask and a cheap plastic cup. "A token of appreciation from the executive producer."

"Thank him for me. It's refreshing to see that he kept his word."

Rick unscrewed the top of the flask and poured the amber liquid into the cup. This was no way to drink good Scotch, but would have to do. "I sure have missed this," he said wistfully, and Zoe had no reason to doubt him.

He gently swirled the liquid clockwise, and took a deep breath. The warden had sprung for the good stuff. Rick guessed it to be Laphroaig, probably sixteen years old. He took a small sip and felt a wonderful burning sensation on his tongue.

It's funny how a taste of good Scotch could take you back in time, to memories long buried. He thought of sitting with his dad in a little Scottish bar when he'd turned twenty-one. They had spent most of the day in the Highlands and most of the night sampling whiskies from the region.

He closed his eyes and took another sip. Vivid memories of Cheryl invaded his mind like an old friend coming by for a visit. They would sit on the deck overlooking the valley and talk about life, politics, and the future while sipping their cocktails of choice: Single malt Scotch for Rick and blackberry margaritas for Cheryl.

"You look lost again," said Zoe. Her words brought him out of his trance-like state.

"I was just thinking about days gone by. With little to look forward to, I seem to retreat more and more into the past."

Zoe frowned. "Don't give up." She tried to smile.

Rick nodded his head and held up his cup. "Would you like a taste?"

"No thanks," she demurred politely. "I can't drink that stuff. Smells like moss."

"That's what I like about it. What do you like to drink?"

"Red wine, or blackberry margaritas, if I'm in the mood."

Rick was taken aback when Zoe mentioned the margaritas. He connected with those who shared his appreciation for interesting libations and exotic foods, dismissing the likes of teetotalers and vegetarians. But the coincidence that she and Cheryl both enjoyed the same concoction and perfume seemed to go beyond having a mere connection; it was a sign. He took another sip of the sacred elixir. "If I ever get out of here, maybe you could join me for a drink."

"It's a date, but don't know what I'll be doing in thirty years." She had a point. She'd be in her seventies and Rick would be pushing daises.

He changed the subject. "Are you going to the bar mitzvah?"

"I work for the man, but we're not close outside of work, so no, I wasn't invited."

"You don't seem heartbroken."

"I'm not a fan of organized religion." They had that in common, too. Rick took a long swallow and savored the taste in his mouth. He turned the flask upside down to show that its contents had been consumed.

"The warden says that you can't tell anyone about this."

"No one would believe me if I did. Thank the warden for me?"

"Yes."

Rick tossed the empty cup and handed her the flask. Their fingers touched again. This time neither of them was in a hurry to end the caress. Their lingering hands did not go unnoticed by Hinkle. "What the hell is going on here?" he demanded to know.

Rick was momentarily shaken. The giant guard could be trouble. If he reported any inappropriate contact with Zoe to the warden, it could put an end to his ever seeing her again.

"Relax, Hinkle. I'm sure the warden wants his flask back."

Zoe took the container and put it back in the bag.

Rick lowered his voice. "I suppose I won't be seeing much of you from now on."

Zoe gave him a mischievous grin. "I wouldn't be so sure."

He felt his pulse quicken. Maybe there was chemistry between them, after all. The possibility of seeing her again would give him something to look forward to.

She reached into her shopping bag again and pulled out a large ream of papers. "I almost forgot." She handed the unbound sheaf to the prisoner. "The warden's script."

Rick thumbed through the pages. "This could take the entire length of my sentence to read."

Zoe laughed out loud. "He's a detail-oriented kind of guy, but it does seem like cruel and unusual punishment . . ."

They gazed at each other for a moment, each wanting to say words that could not be spoken. Zoe turned to Hinkle who was humming a show tune while leaning on the bars that kept the prisoner contained.

"I guess it's time to go back to your old routine. Take your time reading this and check in with the warden . . . Often." She winked before turning to her coworker. "Guard Hinkle, could you escort Rick—I mean the inmate—back to his cell?"

Hinkle approached the prisoner and nudged him out of the makeshift cutting room.

"And send some people to remove all of this equipment," Zoe added.

Rick walked out of solitary confinement clutching Goldberg's script with both hands. He looked back at Zoe as Hinkle led him down the hall.

A bittersweet smile formed on her face like a Francesco Hayez painting. The woman was a work of art.

* * *

This time it was Madonna who contacted the prison during proper business hours to see if she, Paul, and Seth would be able to visit inmate #739365. They had carefully filled out all the appropriate forms and had faxed them to COR. Though she was placed on hold for twelve minutes and transferred three times, someone eventually could tell her that they were cleared to visit.

She thanked the voice on the other end and turned to the brothers. "We're good to go. He's out of solitary and able to receive visitors."

"So nice of them," smirked Paul. "Did they explain what the problem was?"

"No, but let's just move on. And let's leave early on Saturday, okay?"

*   *   *

Hinkle led Rick back to the common area near his cell, where his new friends had been waiting. They gave him a standing ovation.

"Thanks, guys. Miss me?"

"Sure did," said his cellmate Stretch. "Porney held court and now we all feel dirty."

"That's not fair," argued Porney. "I'm not really a storyteller."

"You got that right," said Swindle, who then turned his attention to Rick. "What the hell did you do to get sent to the hole for so long?"

Rick hesitated. "I, um, can't tell you."

Porney took a step towards Rick and sniffed. "Is that alcohol I smell on your breath?"

"State-issued cough drop," retorted Rick, without missing a beat. "Don't get too close, I could be contagious."

They all took two steps backwards.

"Well, welcome home, Rick," said Stretch. "Now, how about another Hollywood story?"

22
BETTE DAVIS TEETH

Kendra was still in pain and scratched at the stitches in her abdomen as if they were bites from Aedes mosquitos. "Shitfuck."

She looked around the empty room, caterwauling and complaining. "For Christ's sake, where is everyone?" Her screaming finally got the attention of an ancient and doddering nurse, who *'rushed'* into the room in what looked like slow motion.

"Problem, Potter?" the old crone casually asked.

"I'm itching like hell, is the problem. I need medication. Morphine, Vicodin, Oxycontin. Any of them."

The nurse checked her chart. "I'm sorry, dear, but you're not scheduled for another dose of ibuprofen for another two hours."

"I'll sue!" Kendra blared out. "What'd you do, steal my kidney? I bet there's a whole black market thing going on here. Just wait 'till I get out. I'll sue all of you."

"I'll be back in a couple of hours. In the meantime, why don't you think about the good things in your life?"

"I would if there were any. Now get the fuck out of here."

The elderly nurse stuck up her middle finger and left the room.

* * *

Morgan was in an uncharacteristically poor mood. "Tell me why we're going here again?"

Macfarlane sighed. "For the hundredth time, because an old detective wants to see us about something he considers important."

"Like we don't have better things to do."

Macfarlane looked at his Barney Fife-like partner. "We really don't have much going on today."

"There's always paperwork. And lunch." Morgan pulled into the lot of the Chatsworth Care Rehabilitation Center. Suddenly, he remembered that the pretty nurse would be there and his mood lightened considerably. "What was that woman's name again? You know, the older one, the nurse."

"Jennifer."

"You didn't happen to notice a ring on her finger, did you?"

"None that I can recall."

For two purportedly top-notch Los Angeles Police Detectives, quite a lot of their recall left something to be desired.

"Let's just stick to business, shall we?" admonished Macfarlane.

"That's the same thing you said to me about Delmarie, and we dated for ten months."

Delmarie was a waitress at a barbeque joint who had been a witness to a stabbing a few years back, and had a brief relationship with the lanky detective. She had been fond of archery and vodka tonics. Macfarlane chose not to respond to his partner, who presently pulled into a space reserved for doctors.

Jen met them at the door with Abby, who had played hooky from school. Morgan's face lit up like a 100-watt bulb.

"Thank you, officers, for coming. You'll need to sign in first." Abby handed the detectives a clipboard, and they quickly scribbled their names and printed their time of arrival in the adjoining box.

Morgan turned to Abby and said; "This is a nice surprise. I thought you had school this morning."

"I'm taking the fifth on that one." She giggled playfully. "C'mon, follow me."

The foursome took the elevator to the third floor, rounded a corner, and approached room 305E. An action music cue and screeching tires blasted through the hallway, suggesting another cop show played at full volume.

"Hi Sam," shouted Jen, as they entered his room. "We've brought a couple of guests with us today."

Morgan put his hands over his ears. "I think they can hear this in Bakersfield," he said, referring to a community that was an hour and a quarter drive away.

Sam smiled and switched off the TV. There was much to discuss with the detectives, and Sam wasn't sure how much energy he could muster. "Thanks for coming. I must be brief."

Jen pulled up three additional folding chairs and they all sat down.

Macfarlane smiled at Beetley. "Hey, Sam. This is my partner Randolph Morgan."

Sam nodded to Morgan.

"I've heard a lot about you," said Morgan. "Glad you're doing better, but you look like shit." The tall toothpick of a detective was tone deaf to any sense of political correctness.

"The Rick Potter case." Sam paused to gather his strength. "I was lead on his first wife's murder and did a little snooping when wife number two met the same fate."

"That case is finished," stated Morgan.

"Let him talk," reprimanded Macfarlane.

Sam continued. "I went to the murder scene and found an unusual gum wrapper across the street." He held up the baggie in a wrinkled hand. "I think this was missed by your team. I saw a man drop an identical wrapper in the courthouse parking lot just after Potter's verdict was read."

"You want us to arrest him for littering?" Everyone ignored Morgan's remark.

Sam continued. "I picked it up, and my lights went out."

"So, you think this gum chewer may have been involved with Tara Potter-Conley-Finley-Goldblatt's murder?" inquired Macfarlane.

"I talked with Rick Potter at length before he was sentenced. He insists that he's innocent, and I believe him," asserted Sam.

There was an awkward silence before Abby spoke up. "Rosey's boyfriend chews this gum nonstop. I did some research. It's imported from Russia and there are only a handful of cases that come to the States every year. Out of those, only two get sent to California. One to San Francisco and one to Northridge, California."

The detectives looked at her, duly impressed.

"I don't get it," said Morgan. "So maybe the wind blew this blue wrapper close to the murder scene."

Sam tried to find his words. "Then how did it get to the court-house?" he asked, at last. "Look, the gum chewer *lives* with Rosey Kern. Her daughter, Kendra, was convicted of murdering Rick's wife. They knew each other."

Macfarlane was trying to process this information. He turned to Abby. "Tell me about this boyfriend."

"He scares the shit out of me." Abby saw the surprised look on everyone's face. "Oh, sorry for the language. He's Russian, doesn't talk much, and strong."

A light turned on in Macfarlane's head. "Is he short, bald, with beady eyes?"

"That's him," she assented.

"The guy from the tavern," said Morgan. He may have been slow on the uptake, but was now starting to get the picture. He continued, "A violent man. The nerd he beat up is trying to place a restraining order on him."

Macfarlane turned to Abby. "What's this guy's name?"

"Ollie. No idea what his last name is."

Sam listened to all this and said weakly, "You need to investigate him for Tara . . . What's her name's . . . Murder."

* * *

Rick had his group in stitches. "—And then she started to talk funny like her teeth needed an adjustment."

His audience listened with the rapt attention of kindergarteners at a Reading Rainbow.

Rick was telling the story of cutting Bette Davis's last film, *The Wicked Stepmother*. "She had been attempting a comeback, but was insecure and nearly deaf at this late stage of life. She had asked to preview the dailies to see if her performance was still up to her high standards. The director had me assemble the raw footage, but insisted that I remove any egregious takes. During the screening she noticed that some of the footage was missing. The old diva rose from her chair and shouted, 'Mr. Editor. You have been manipulating the rushes!'"

"We convened in the lobby as Ms. Davis continued to rant. That was when her dentures flew out of her mouth and onto my sneakers."

The normally dour Swindle doubled over in laughter.

23

ON THE ROAD AND
PASTRAMI SANDWICHES

"So, what do you think?" asked Morgan as he sat with his partner at Brent's, a Jewish delicatessen located a few miles south of the Chatsworth Care Rehab Facility.

"I think Sam means well, but the evidence in that case was overwhelming."

"I was talking about the menu."

Macfarlane sighed and perused the pages, which were more like a book than a menu.

The veteran waitress arrived wearing comfortable shoes and sporting a mustard stain on her apron. "What'll it be, fellas?" she asked with the bored inflection of a cop handing out a citation.

Macfarlane ordered corned beef on white bread with mayonnaise, while Morgan selected a chef salad.

"Why would you order salad at a deli?"

"Just craving some romaine and tomatoes."

"What kind of craving is that?"

"I have a highly sensitive palate. Plus, I'm watching my boyish figure."

Morgan was a tall drink of water with a body that resembled a stick. He couldn't have tipped the scales at 150 pounds if his pockets were stuffed with coins.

"About the Potter case. You think all this is a waste of time?"

Macfarlane rubbed his chin. "I guess it wouldn't hurt to take another look at the files. We're not that busy."

*   *   *

Kendra was cranky: not an unusual state for her. She had been escorted from the prison infirmary to the mess hall. The stitches on the lower right side of her abdomen itched like an untreated rash, and she was craving a corned beef sandwich much like the one a certain detective had ordered at a deli, some 240 miles away. Instead, she got something that resembled Hungarian goulash. She studied the blob on her plate as her only friend June took a seat beside her.

"Hey, you're back." June studied Kendra's pale face. "You don't look so good."

"I had surgery. I didn't even know I was sick."

"I hate when that happens. Were you able to come up with a plan? If you did, I'm all in."

"I was too busy almost dying."

Kendra turned her attention to the meal in front of her. She studied her plate.

"What the fuck is this?"

"Saturday surprise. It's not as bad as it looks."

Kendra was doubtful, but hungry. She picked up a portion of the white goo with her plastic fork and took a nibble.

"Shitfuck. I wouldn't serve this to a starving child."

"Then can I have yours? I'm famished."

Kendra noticed tiny tracks in her mush and pushed her plate towards her friend. "This may put *you* in the infirmary."

She watched as June started poking into the concoction.

"What are you doing?"

"Looking for bugs."

Finally satisfied that her meal was generally free of insects, and any other form of protein for that matter, she dug in and took a big bite. "Not so bad."

June started stuffing her face as Kendra, feeling nauseous, threw up on her plate.

* * *

The weather outside the aging Honda was a scorching 97 degrees, but inside it was a comfortable 72. The car was slowly falling apart, but the air conditioner worked like gangbusters.

Paul was hunched behind the wheel, with Madonna riding shotgun. Seth and Noga were both sound asleep in the back seats—Noga clutching her Beach Barbie Doll in her hands like a misshapen miniature pillow. They were two hours into the long journey to visit Rick at the California State Prison, Corcoran. This was their third attempt to visit their dad, and so far the end result had been a waste of two tanks of gas and an outlay of twenty dollars to rent a slab of asphalt for a total of ten minutes.

The previous evening Noga had put up such a fight that the group had no choice but to bring her along. She was a strong-minded child who had argued in both Yiddish and English, and with the fury of a Congressman during an impeachment trial.

"How're you doing, babe?" asked Madonna as she ran her fingers through Paul's hair. "Want me to take over?"

"No, I got this." The radio was turned off so it wouldn't disturb the dreamers in the back.

Northward eighteen-wheelers bound with assorted cargo sped by at speeds of up to 90 miles per hour.

Paul shook his head. "What's their fucking hurry?"

"Let them get speeding tickets," said Madonna.

They drove in silence for a few minutes before Madonna mused, "I can't imagine what your dad is going through. Locked up with murderers, rapists, and politicians. It's bound to change him."

Paul continued driving in moderate traffic. "I know."

Paul was not a big talker.

A thought had been running through Madonna's mind and she decided to share it. "Maybe you should have told those cops that you were there the night of the murder. That you saw Tara screaming at your dad as he left her townhouse."

Paul weighed her suggestion. "I wanted to, but his lawyer said that it would look like an obvious lie—a son trying to help his father. I'm not sure about this ambulance chaser, but he also said that it would place me at the crime scene and make me an accessory to murder. It made sense and dad agreed it was best to keep me out of it."

"But, what could it hurt? Especially now?"

"What are you saying?"

"I'm saying that maybe you should contact those detectives. Tell them what you saw," she implored.

Paul considered her words. "I think it's six months too late."

An uncomfortable silence followed. He looked straight ahead, but could practically feel her stare reproaching him for his lack of fortitude. He stole a quick glance to his right to take her measure before speaking. "But if you think it's the right thing to do . . ."

"Then it's settled." Madonna moved closer to Paul, who put his arm around her.

"How'd I get so lucky to find you?"

"I'm not sure, but you hit the jackpot." She rested her head on Paul's shoulder.

24
THE PLOT THICKENS

Sam was improving incrementally every day, but it was a slow process, and the retired detective was frustrated. He was anxious to learn whether Macfarlane and Morgan had followed up on the gum wrapper lead he had provided them with. He couldn't be of much help lying flat on his back in a rehab facility inhabited by the aged and infirm; in other words, by people just like him.

He picked up the remote control and turned on the flat screen that hung on the wall opposite the bed. He raised the volume to level eleven and flipped channels before settling on a cable news program. The entire facility listened along with him. It was hard work being old.

Sam cursed as he watched in horror the unfolding of another school shooting, this time in Philadelphia, PA. When was the government going to do something about guns? *Certainly not in my lifetime*, he thought.

He discovered that a lot of bad things had gone on while he lay unconscious. History was bound to repeat itself, and people never seemed to learn from it. For the first time since emerging from his coma, he wanted a drink. Maybe he could convince the nice aide to sneak him some hooch.

* * *

"Are we there yet?" asked a groggy six-year-old while rubbing sleep out of her dough-brown eyes.

Madonna looked at the GPS on her phone before answering. "Siri says about ten more minutes."

"I need to go potty."

Seth felt the same bodily urge. "Me, too."

Paul nodded from behind the wheel. "We should probably fill up anyway."

The Honda pulled off the freeway and into a Mobile station that doubled as a minimart.

Madonna, Noga, and Seth all headed to the restrooms while Paul filled the tank with regular, the whole time thinking about what he would say to his dad. He considered mentioning his plan to talk with the detectives, but dismissed the thought. It might give him some kind of false hope.

The truth was that his dad would probably die in prison and they all had to come to terms with that. And the sooner the better. Hope was reserved for the religious, or the naïve, and his father was neither.

Life had thrown a lot of curve balls to the Potter family over the years, but they became more like wild pitches the day Nate brought Kendra and Bryan to live with them. Since that evil woman entered their lives, everything had turned to shit. He could never forgive her, or his older brother for that matter.

Seth finished doing his business and went to a less-than-clean sink to wash his hands. Fearing germs just from being near the latrine, he lathered up before rinsing, only to find the paper towel dispenser empty.

"Shit." He wiped his hands on his pants and went out to peruse the minimart for snacks.

* * *

Nate had the day off and was now occupying a barstool at his favorite Korean sports bar, Jug-Jug. He was sipping on a rum and Coke, noshing on stale peanuts, and listening to more of Marshall's sexual exploits.

"So, she was older, maybe sixty, but she looked younger; at least in the dark. She thought I was Johnny Depp, and I didn't want to disappoint her, so I played along."

Nate took another fistful of nuts.

"She handcuffs me to the bed and walks away. I wait, thinking this was kind of kinky, but she was gone a long time. I started to worry. What if she never came back? I didn't even know her name."

Nate raised an eyebrow. Marshall continued: "About an hour later, I heard the front door open, and she walked in with a bottle of tequila. She said, 'Sorry mate, I had a craving.'"

"She poured tequila down my throat and eventually uncuffed me. I got totally shitfaced. I don't remember a fucking thing after that, but I was sore for three days."

Marshall took a sip of his rusty nail.

"I wonder what she's doing right now," said Nate, more to his drink than to his friend.

"Probably whipping some asshole who was stupid enough to let her chain him up."

"I was talking about Kendra."

"Oh . . . I knew that," noted Marshall, unconvincingly.

Nate was feeling lonely and more morose than usual.

"How much longer is she in for?" asked Marshall.

"A year and change. I'm not even sure I want her to come back."

Marshall didn't know how to respond to that remark, so he didn't.

*   *   *

As the weary travelers exited the freeway and took the long road towards the prison, it appeared as a citadel: massive, stark, and cold.

Paul pulled up to the familiar parking kiosk and grabbed the ticket that stuck out like a dry tongue. "We should start collecting these. Maybe with enough of them we can win a toaster."

This time the parking lot was full and Paul had to drive around to find a spot. When he did, they all exited the car and moved towards the entrance. Noga looked with wide-eyed awe at the gray walls, the guard tower, and the endless rolls of barbed wire. She held her bikini-clad doll tight.

"I don't like this place."

Seth took her by the hand and gently squeezed it. "Me either," he murmured.

At the sally port, they waited their turn in line to pass through the metal detector. They made it through without setting off any alarms and were then patted down by serious-looking men in uniforms.

Noga giggled, "That tickles."

Just ahead, the same obnoxious sergeant was manning the same cluttered desk. Seth handed Crawford the forms and waited while he looked them over. "This all looks in order."

"Third times a charm," said Paul.

Crawford sneered at him before picking up his phone. "Are you going to be trouble?"

"No, he's not." Madonna took Paul by the arm. "Where do we go?"

Crawford motioned with a jerk of his head to a far door. As they walked past the guard they heard his booming voice call out, "Stop right there."

The Potter clan stopped in their tracks and turned around.

Crawford pointed to Noga and said, "What's the kid holding?"

"That's my dolly," said a defiant Noga.

"Can't bring that in with you. It could contain contraband."

Seth was appalled. "You can't be serious. It's a little girl's doll for God's sake."

Crawford wasn't moved. "There could be drugs, a phone, or a weapon inside that doll. You can trash it over there," he said, pointing to a large trash can, "or go back to your car and put it away. And by the way, the doll's clothes are inappropriate attire for this facility."

Paul turned and looked at the long line of visitors waiting in line behind them. "It's Beach Barbie and what's wrong with the doll wearing a bathing suit?"

People in line were beginning to get restless, and Crawford was losing his patience. "What's it gonna be? Either toss the Beach Barbie, or take it back to your vehicle."

Noga gave the guard some major stink-eye before blurting out, *"Meshuggeneh, Shmegegge!"*

Crawford looked to Madonna for a translation. "You don't want to know," she said before taking Noga by the hand. "C'mon guys. Let's go back to the car."

Paul gave Crawford his dirtiest look and asked, "Can we skip the line when we come back?"

Crawford took great pleasure in saying no.

The group retraced their steps and placed Beach Barbie in the car. Eventually, they were back inside the prison lobby where they patiently waited in line again. When they reached the front, Seth handed their paperwork to Crawford.

He took his time looking over the form. "I guess you're good to go," said Crawford. "Next."

Seth whispered to Paul. "I'm not tipping him on the way out."

They passed through the door that had been indicated by the sour sergeant and into a room that was divided down the middle by a glass partition. Men with long guns secured the half that was filled with friends and family of the interned. A handful of inmates sat on the prisoners' side of the partition, speaking on phones to the visitors seated opposite them. The Potter clan looked through the enormous glass panel, scanning the other side of the room for their dad.

Noga was the first to spot him being escorted to an empty chair.

"I see him, I see him." She pointed to her grandfather, whose face beamed at the sight of her.

Noga ran towards him, took a seat on a plastic chair, and lifted the phone.

"Grandpa, you look . . . Older."

You've got to love a child's honesty.

"I *am* older . . . I've missed you," said Rick, his voice badly filtered through the receiver.

"I want you to come home with us." Noga started to tear up.

"I wish I could. Maybe one day."

"Please . . .?"

Seth gently nudged Noga out of the chair and took the phone. "Hey, Pops. How are they treating you?"

"Could be worse. I've lost weight and still have my prison virginity."

Seth smiled. "At least that's something, right?"

Rick grinned in response. "Yeah, it's something."

"This is our third attempt to see you. You would not believe all the red tape we have had to go through."

"It's great to see you. I know it's a long drive."

Paul tapped Seth's shoulder and took the phone. "Hey, Dad. When we came last time they told us you were in solitary confinement. What'd you do?" He looked for bruises on his father's face. "You didn't get into a brawl did you?"

"Actually, I was doing the warden a favor."

"You can't go anywhere without people hitting you up for favors," jested Paul.

Rick nodded. "You're right about that."

Madonna took the receiver from Paul and gently elbowed him out of the way. Rick smiled at the pretty blonde girl that he had once picked up hitchhiking on his way to Palm Springs. They had struck up a quick friendship and he thought that she and Paul would get along. He was right.

"We've missed you." Madonna tried hard to put on a brave face.

"Thanks for coming. We don't see many women in this joint."

Madonna tried to smile, but her heart wasn't cooperating. Seeing him like this was just too painful. His prison jumpsuit was ill fitting and his eyes looked empty. It was as if his spirit had gone AWOL. Fortunately, Noga impatiently grabbed the phone.

"Grandpa, I love you."

Rick smiled fondly down at his little granddaughter. A droplet of fluid formed in his eye.

"I love you, too."

25

DEPRESSION AND DOUGHNUTS

Teddy Williams peeked through the blinds in his living room and surveyed his small front yard and the street behind it. No sign of the lunatic who had threatened him at the tavern and assaulted him in his own home.

His Costco security system had been professionally installed, and new and horribly expensive locks had replaced the old ones. Still, he didn't feel protected.

His attacker was obviously deranged and, in fact, no amount of security could convince Teddy that he was safe. He realized that a restraining order was just a piece of paper and wouldn't stop an intruder if one really wanted to hurt him.

Firearms were not an option either. In his 70 years on earth, Teddy had never held a gun. They scared him like a new tax initiative.

His anxiety caused him to pop an Anxozen and swallow it dry.

He turned on the television and watched the aftermath of yet another mass shooting: this time at an upscale restaurant in Peoria, Illinois. Six were pronounced dead at the scene, including a four-year-old girl. Three others, diners at the establishment, were seriously wounded before they could even finish their dessert.

What was happening to this country? Teddy shared the same concerns that an elderly recovering ex-detective had. The insurance agent got up and checked his security monitor. The screen was divided into eight sections, each with a different view of both the outside and inside of his house. Everything looked normal, but looks could be deceiving. He was aware that his nemesis knew where he lived and could be waiting for him just outside the camera's view.

* * *

Kendra and June were finishing lunch. Or more to the point, June was finishing both their lunches.

Ever since her infirmary stay, Kendra had had no appetite. It was more than just a dislike for the food; she was mired in a depression that was escalating and would go undiagnosed anytime in the near future.

June looked at her and held up a forkful of mush. "You sure you won't just have a bite? You're getting so thin."

"I'm not hungry," barked Kendra.

"How about painting another clown? That always cheers you up."

"I'm clowned out."

Kendra got up and left June alone at the table.

* * *

On Monday morning, at Madonna's urging, Paul reluctantly drove to the Devonshire Station to talk with the detectives. Paul was no fan of cops, who had locked up his dad for life and had recently presented him with a citation for going five miles over the speed limit.

Police shootings of unarmed citizens were now commonplace, and nobody seemed to be doing anything about it. Body cameras were a good idea, but when cops turned them off, bad things seemed to happen. Coincidence? Paul didn't think so.

The inmate's son pulled up to the station in his Ford F-150 and trudged to the entrance. A banner invited him to a community breakfast this coming Sunday. There was no chance he'd attend such an event, but at least they were trying.

He thought this particular mission was pointless, but his father *was* in prison, and if there were even a remote possibility that he could help, he would try. Madonna's intuitions were usually spot-on.

Paul was an imposing figure at 6'4," and as he walked into the station, Perez, the desk sergeant on duty, was somewhat taken aback by his looming presence. "Can I help you?" he asked, looking up at the towering entrant.

"I'd like to talk to the detectives who worked the Rick Potter case a few months back."

Sergeant Perez nodded. He was not the first person to come in recently asking for them. He found this peculiar because that case had been wrapped up months ago.

"And you are—?"

"Rick Potter's son, Paul."

Perez looked at the powerfully built man carefully. Paul was wearing a *Cowboy Junkies* tee shirt that stretched across a muscular chest. Tan cargo shorts showed no sign of a weapon. Nonetheless, the son of a convicted murderer entering a police station looking for the detectives that sent his father away smacked of trouble.

"Have a seat and I'll see if they're in," instructed Perez. As Paul complied, the officer picked up a phone, spoke for a few seconds, and then stood up. "I'm afraid I'm going to have to pat you down. Police policy."

Paul put up his hands and spread his legs apart. The guy was just doing his job. Perez finished his brief examination and said, "Follow me."

Paul followed the sergeant through the halls and into the bullpen.

"That's them over there," said Perez, pointing a finger in the detectives' direction.

Paul felt self-conscious as he walked toward the men. It was as if the whole room was watching.

The detectives instantly saw Paul approach; they couldn't miss the imposing figure that advanced closer to their desks. He stopped and said, "Thanks for seeing me. My name is Paul Potter."

Macfarlane stood up and extended a hand. "I'm Detective Macfarlane, and this is Detective Morgan. I think we briefly spoke with you during the investigation."

Paul had no recollection of having ever met these guys. He was probably still in shock when that may have occurred. He shook hands with both men and pulled up a cheap chair.

"What can we do for you?" asked Macfarlane.

"It's the investigation into my dad's case I want to talk about. I have some information."

That certainly caught their attention. The detectives looked at each other. *First Sam Beetley, and now this*, was the thought that had to have crossed their minds simultaneously.

Morgan set his cheeseburger on the desk as Macfarlane leaned in to Paul. "Talk to us."

Paul opened up, as he never thought he would. "The night of the murder I followed my father to an Italian restaurant. He was meeting his ex-wife for dinner."

"And you followed him because . . .?" asked Morgan.

"Because Pops was not in good shape. He had gone to Palm Springs, where he'd been mugged. He was beaten up pretty good. The reason he wanted to see Tara was that he believed she killed my mom years ago. He wanted to confront her and find out for sure."

The two detectives looked at each other again: this was news to them.

"Go on," urged Macfarlane.

"I watched them come out of the restaurant and get into their cars. Dad followed her to her townhouse and I followed him. I pulled over to the curb and waited. I was worried for my dad's safety. He's older and, like I said, he was in bad physical shape. If Tara *had* murdered my mother, he could have been in danger. He was inside her place for about fifteen minutes. I was about to check on him when I saw him come out. He was holding a napkin to his face and she was screaming, 'you'll never prove it, asshole.' He got into his car and I followed him home."

Paul paused, looking from one cop to the other. "Tara was pissed but very much alive when he left."

Macfarlane had been taking notes and now looked up. "Why didn't you say anything before?" It was a valid question.

"I wanted to. I told dad what I just told you, and he discussed it with his lawyer. I think he earned his diploma online. He said that it would look like a desperate attempt to help my father and it would have given him a motive for killing her. The lawyer said that I could be charged as an accessory. Dad didn't want me involved in any way."

Paul had said his piece in one breath and now fell silent.

"Did you notice anyone else that night in front of her townhouse?" Morgan's interest had perked up.

"There were several cars parked on both sides of the street, but I didn't see anything suspicious."

The detectives exchanged looks, their thoughts synchronized like picture and sound in one of Rick's edited movies. This fresh account, along with Sam Beetley's wrapper clue, suggested this case needed fresh scrutiny.

Macfarlane stood up. "I'm glad you came in. Can't promise anything, but we'll poke around a bit."

"Thanks, appreciate it."

Paul didn't have much faith in these two, but he had done all that he could and Madonna would be pleased.

Macfarlane and Morgan watched Paul leave. The information they had been presented with was impossible to ignore. The mustachioed cop remained seated while the string bean took a bite of his burger and then walked to the office snack station where he poured a cup of old coffee. He returned to his desk and said, "I think Adam Sandler is highly overrated."

"Where did that come from?" Macfarlane wanted to know.

"I just don't find him funny, that's all. And by the way, the Potter case was settled months ago."

Macfarlane took a deep breath before responding. "Do you believe the kid?"

Morgan nodded his head. "I do."

"Okay. Let's start going through all our interviews. I don't recall ever talking to this Russian gum chewer. Then let's pay another visit to Sam at the rehabilitation center."

26

ABBY THE SPY

Rick Potter was startled from a deep slumber by a stray basketball bouncing off the side of his head. He jerked awake, blinked a couple times, trying to remember where he was. Then succeeded, to his chagrin; he was sitting on a bench in the prison exercise yard.

A handful of inmates were engaged in a very physical game of basketball, pushing and shoving, shouting and swearing at each other as if they were at any city park in the country. Other prisoners strained at heavy weights, or jogged in circles around the concrete track.

Warden Goldberg's script lay open in Rick's lap. It was a tedious 219 page tome that appeared to be a whimsical account of a dog's life on the streets. At first Rick thought that it was intended to be a comedy, but it was hard to tell. Whatever, Rick knew from experience that a feature script should be an economical 90 to 110 pages long. This thing was *War and Peace*. He had only gotten to page fifteen and he had already given up taking notes and had fallen asleep twice.

Rick knew he would have to be diplomatic in his critique of the warden's work. Writers are a particularly sensitive lot, and this one could make his time here in prison decidedly more difficult.

His first note to the warden would be to trim about a hundred pages off the manuscript. This could easily be accomplished by simply editing out all the stage directions, scene and character descriptions, camera cues and miscellaneous and sundry extraneous minutia used to describe the action.

Rick yawned, sighed, and tried to get back to reading. His eyes wandered to the other jailbirds, getting their exercise. They seemed so young. What had they done to be sent here? Would their futures be as bleak as his? He knew that he should engage in some sort of physical activity, but his heart simply wasn't in it. After all, what would be the point: a healthier body just to spend more years behind bars? At 68 he was one of the oldest inmates at COR, and had little hope of ever leaving. Not alive, anyway.

*   *   *

Rosey was in a funk. She was still pissed at Ollie for the altercation with one of her best customers and hadn't spoken to him in a week. Teddy Williams had not returned, and now she was reticent to interact with customers, fearing another outburst from her "boyfriend."

The tavern was still popular and making money, but the restaurant business was volatile. Rosey's Tavern was known as a fun family restaurant, and news of violence could hurt her business: and word traveled faster than ants at a picnic in this part of the valley.

She was fuming at Ollie and melancholy about Kendra withering away in prison. It had been some time since anyone had heard from her, and with Kendra that could mean anything. Or nothing. But it usually meant *something*, and more often than not, that something wasn't good.

Nate seemed down in the dumps and who could blame him?

It had been weeks since Rosey had seen her grandson Bryan and his bride, Mona, and she decided that a gathering of her extended clan was in order. She got on the horn and invited them to dinner.

Remarkably, all were available on such short notice. The sound of a free meal at Rosey's Tavern was too good to pass up.

The only person she hadn't spoken with was Ollie. She was still angry with him, and his behavior had become unpredictable. In the end, she decided that Ollie was family, in his own peculiar way, and decided to include him. She punched in Ollie's number and left a message when he failed to answer.

* * *

Macfarlane and Morgan had spent the last three hours in the evidence locker going over the volumes of paperwork collected from the Potter murder investigation. They reviewed interviews with Rosey, Nate, the Potter boys, Mona, and Abby. None of them contributed anything of value to the probe. The mysterious Russian had not been interviewed at all.

"I won't lose sleep over his conviction," said Morgan. "Looks cut and dry."

"The thing that bothers me most," Macfarlane replied, "is that his were the only fingerprints found on the murder weapon."

"Yeah, I never bought his story that he used that ice pick to chip ice for an inferior blended Scotch. But then again, I'm not much of a drinker."

"Let's talk to Sam and explain that we reviewed the files, and that our conclusion remains the same."

They returned the boxes to gather dust in the precinct's basement: a morgue of paperwork that chronicled the sad demise of unfortunate victims.

* * *

By seven-fifteen that evening, Rosey and family were sitting in a back booth at the Tavern, drinking wine and munching on breadsticks. Abby and Jeff sipped diet Cokes and talked about their upcoming senior prom. Nate groused that the backup bartender had forgotten to put alcohol in his drink. Rosey was in deep conversation with Bryan and Mona, who looked very much in love. There was no mistaking the sparkle in their eyes, and Rosey thought that they were the only truly happy members of a dysfunctional family.

The only person not engaged in conversation was Ollie. He had arrived late, but had already consumed his second vodka rocks, with no complaints about the amount of alcohol in *his* glass.

Two gum wrappers lay like drowned soldiers by his water glass, the blue color contrasting nicely against a tablecloth of white linen. The wrappers caught Abby's attention and she made an executive decision to try and swipe one of them to show the detectives more direct evidence. She felt like an undercover operative and hoped to gather additional information about the mysterious man seated next to her.

"You're always so quiet," she said to Ollie. He half-smiled and nodded his head.

Abby persisted. "Where are you from?"

Rosey's internal alarm system went off. She knew that Ollie was a private man who revealed little. "He's from Russia and not very talkative."

Ollie took a sip of his Tito's on the rocks, glad that Rosey had intervened.

"I don't even know your last name," said Abby in a casual tone of voice.

"Perkovich," he said before standing up. "Excuse me."

Ollie walked toward the men's room.

Rosey wanted to discourage any more questioning before Ollie got angry. "Honey, Ollie is very private. You should leave him alone."

Abby would have to be more careful. There was more to working undercover than she had realized. "Oh, sorry. I was just trying to be friendly."

Rosey summoned the waitress and ordered for the table; a veritable smorgasbord of the best items on the menu. With Ollie temporarily MIA, Abby slowly inched her hand towards the gum wrappers. Sweat formed on her forehead. She looked around the table to see if anyone was looking in her direction. The coast seemed clear. Her fingers closed in now, perhaps two inches away. This was her chance. Suddenly, the sound of breaking glass by the bar caught the table's attention, and heads turned in that direction.

Abby deftly placed her hand over the paper and slid it toward her. Her heart raced as she carefully deposited her treasure into her back pocket. She used a napkin to wipe away the beads of perspiration that were multiplying on her face. She felt like a spy who had just gotten the goods from a Russian asset. Maybe she could pen a dossier.

She turned her attention to Nate who looked like he'd rather be anywhere else. "So—Nate. How's Kendra doing?"

Jefferson winced at her question. Everyone knew not to bring up the subject of Nate's wife.

"No idea," Nate grumbled.

Rosey decided to intervene again. "Abby, try the rumaki: we make it fresh."

Ollie returned to his seat, reached into his pocket and pulled out a fresh stick of gum. His habit was as bad as a heroin addict in need of a fix. He placed the wrapper on the table and did a double take. One of the wrappers was missing. He nonchalantly looked under the table and around the floor. Where had it gone?

His eyes settled on Abby who quickly turned away.

Ignoring Rosey's hints, and wanting more information, she continued her conversation with Nate. "Do you ever talk to your dad?"

"No, he's dead to me." Nate belted down the remainder of his cocktail. Jefferson shook his head.

This time Mona interceded. "Abby, why don't you tell everyone about your job?" To the table she added, "Abby's been working part time in a nursing home."

"Mom, it's not a nursing home. It's the Chatsworth Care Rehabilitation Facility. We care for people that need physical help. Hopefully they can recover enough to move back home or to an assisted living community."

Rosey was impressed. "That's wonderful, Abby. You can make a difference in their lives."

"There's one patient I'm particularly fond of. An old detective named Sam Beetley."

Rosey's ears perked up like a Doberman Pincher sensing danger. "Why does that name ring a bell?"

Abby turned to Nate. "He worked on your step-mom's murder case all those years ago."

"That bastard," groused Nate.

"He also looked into your mom's . . . He thinks your father is innocent."

Ollie froze, his eyes narrowing. What was this girl saying? Who was this retired detective stirring up trouble? Ollie had gotten away with murder and Potter was rotting in prison. He took another sip of Tito's Homemade Vodka, glaring at Abby, weighing every word she said.

27

A DRY BEAR CLAW
AND A PLAN

Rick Potter was in the prison cafeteria picking at his shit on a shingle—slang for chipped beef on toast. That particular delicacy was a California prison mainstay. He looked at his breakfast and was reminded of the time he threw up in Moscow's Red Square when he traveled through Eastern Europe between high school and the rest of his life. That seemed like a hundred years ago. Where had the time gone?

Just then a great shadow cast over him blocking the artificial light. Huge Hinkle placed a hand the size of a catcher's mitt on Rick's shoulder. "Warden wants to see you."

Rick wondered if the warden had another project for him. It didn't matter; whatever he wanted to see him about, it would be another chance to see Zoe.

* * *

Detective Morgan had spent 25 minutes at Sally's Doughnuts trying to decide which of the oval fat-helpers to bring to Chatsworth Care. Morgan had a sweet tooth, and they had all looked wonderful. By the time he picked up Macfarlane at his apartment, the dozen doughnuts he'd selected were down to ten.

Macfarlane saw the pink pastry box on the console. "What's all this?"

Morgan bit into a gooey jelly glazed doughnut. "I picked up a dozen doughnuts on the way over. I thought maybe we should bring something to Sam and the nurses at the rehab center. I never like to arrive at a function empty handed."

"There's two missing. Couldn't you wait?" asked Macfarlane.

"Obviously not. I skipped dinner last night and was starving. There's still more than enough for all of us."

"That's not the point. Now it looks like we're bringing leftovers."

"You get that from Martha Stewart?" sniped Morgan.

Macfarlane shook his head and turned on the radio. A country tune pierced the speakers. "How can you listen to this?"

"Do you really want to know?"

"As a matter of fact, no. Hand me a glazed will you?"

Morgan responded, "That's kind of hypocritical don't you think?"

"What are you talking about?"

"You just Martha Stewart-ed me for pilfering a couple of doughnuts, and now you're doing the same thing."

Macfarlane made one last point. "Once you open the box the gift rule doesn't apply."

Morgan conceded the point.

*   *   *

Inside the rehab facility, Sam was watching television at his usual high decibel level. Canned laughter echoed in the hallway.

Jen covered her ears and breezed into his room. "How's our patient doing this morning?"

Sam shut off the TV and turned to the attractive nurse. "I'm still alive . . . I think."

She laughed and took the chair next to him.

"Really, how do you feel?"

"Better every day. In a week I'll start training for the Olympics."

Jen didn't believe an Olympic event was in his future, but he did have color in his face and his speech was improving. Before she could say anything else, the two detectives entered the room, a pink cardboard box in Macfarlane's arms like he was holding an infant.

His partner was munching on a doughnut: colorful sprinkles decorated his tie like dandruff on a suit. "I hope you're hungry," said Morgan.

He took the box from Macfarlane and placed it on the nightstand. The sweet, sugary smell filled the room. "Trust me, these are the best in town. We cops know our doughnuts."

He opened the box and pointed to the government-mandated calorie disclosures with the gesture of a game show model showing a contestant what they had just won.

"Sorry, but those will go directly to my hips," said Jen.

Morgan eyed her figure. "You could use a little extra padding, if you don't mind my saying."

Macfarlane got to the point. "Sam, we went over the Potter files again. Couldn't find anything in there to change our opinion."

"The Russian?" inquired Sam.

"He was never interviewed."

Sam's astonishment was apparent.

"But there is something else," said Morgan.

Sam scooted up in his bed.

Macfarlane took over. "Potter's kid came to see us. The tall one. Told us that he had followed his father the night of the murder. Said his dad came out of the victim's residence with Tara screaming, 'You'll never prove it.'"

Sam's head fell back on his pillow. He struggled to get his words out. "You must talk to the Russian." If the son's story could be corroborated, it was game changing.

Jen peeked inside the pink box and extracted a jelly doughnut.

"Those are fantastic," said Morgan, who stuck his hand in the box and came up with a bear claw. He sniffed it before taking a bite.

Meanwhile, Macfarlane was thoughtful. One could not dismiss the intuition of a detective who had spent half a lifetime on the force. They sensed things others could not. He turned to his junior partner. "What do you think?"

"I think the bear claw is a little dry." Then, seeing the look on Macfarlane's face, he quickly added, "Let's talk to this Russkie."

Just then Abby burst into the room and all eyes turned in her direction. "What'd I miss?"

Morgan's face lit up like a match. "A jelly, a sprinkled, and a bear claw. But we saved some for you." He held up the box. "Have a doughnut?"

"Thanks. Maybe later."

She fumbled inside her purse. "I have something for you." Suddenly, like a sorceress pulling a lucky charm out of thin air, she produced the purloined gum wrapper from the night before. "Look what I got! I swiped this from Ollie last night. And that's not all."

She turned to the roomful of astonished faces, with a proud smile. "I found out his last name is Perkovich. He's been living with Rosey for about a year. We were all at dinner and I told my Uncle Nate that you thought that his dad might be innocent." She grinned. "You should have seen the expression on Ollie's face. He looked like he had just taken a big bite of some rotten borscht."

Beetley looked concerned. "I wish you wouldn't have said anything. He could be dangerous."

Abby seemed taken aback. "I just wanted to help."

Sam closed his eyes, physically drained. The bright spark in him was dimming like a tired light bulb. He had nothing left.

Morgan finished writing Ollie's last name in his notepad. "Well, now we have a name. That ballplayer can take out his restraining order."

28

GRILLED REUBENS AND WAR AND PEACE

Rick followed Hinkle to the warden's office.

At the sound of the door opening, Zoe looked up from her computer and grinned. She had on green eye shadow that accented her coffee-colored eyes. An overhead light highlighted her jet-black hair.

Rick was momentarily tongue-tied. "Um . . . Hi."

"Hello."

"It's good to see you."

Zoe's smile widened. "Back at you. The warden would like a word."

"Let me guess. He needs a wedding video? Or a bris video?"

"What's a bris?"

"Never mind." It was obvious Zoe was not up on her Jewish customs, and he didn't think this was the time to expand upon her education about a ritual reserved for Jewish males at birth.

She smiled anyway. "I'll let him know you're here." She pressed a digit on the landline and announced that Rick had arrived.

"Send him in," said a raspy voice on speaker.

"I'd rather stay here," said Rick.

And who could blame him? Zoe's presence was bewitching.

Zoe began to blush. "I'd like that . . . But you'd better go in."

Rick sighed and kept his eyes on her as he entered the warden's office.

Goldberg was seated behind his desk, putting pen to paper. He signed his name with a flourish, took off his glasses, and motioned for the prisoner to sit.

"I want to thank you again for the bar mitzvah video," he began. "It was a huge hit. I hope you don't mind that I took credit for your work."

Rick reflexively bridled at the revelation, but quickly came to his senses: it was, after all, just a bar mitzvah video, not an episode of prime-time television viewed by millions. Besides, this wasn't the first such usurpation of its kind.

"I had an assistant editor named Sarah who did the same thing. It worked out very well . . . For her."

"Have you had time to read my script?"

"I managed to make some time in my busy schedule, but I'm a long way from finishing it."

When the warden didn't respond, Rick continued. "So far, I can tell you that the page count is too long. If you shorten it, get to the meat of each scene, it will help immensely."

"I see. But the thing is, I need to describe everything in detail or the audience would never understand the subtext."

This guy had obviously taken a course in script writing that had gone completely over his head.

Goldberg thought that if he could only get his script into the right hands, he could leave the penitentiary and start accepting awards.

Rick tried to lighten his criticism. "Story-wise, I find the subject matter . . . Interesting. I guess a homeless dog rummaging for food in trash cans and shitting on lawns, is . . . Ah . . ." Rick searched his mind for the right word. After all, he didn't want his review of only part of the warden's script to sound completely negative. " . . . Promising."

The warden's face frowned. "Why don't you reserve judgment until you've read the entire script? After all, I did get an 'A' for that work." Rick blinked. An 'A' for this crap? Where did this guy go to school, some junior collage specializing in animal behavior?

The warden wasn't finished. "Why don't you continue reading. And study it carefully. I know that prison life can be a distraction."

Goldberg stood up and put out a hand. "By the way, how was that Scotch?"

"Heavenly. Thank you."

With that, Rick left his office and returned to Zoe's outer sanctuary. The words that he'd been keeping himself from uttering finally spilled out.

"You look beautiful today."

Zoe's face turned red. "Just today?"

Now it was Rick's turn to blush.

Hinkle lumbered in to escort the inmate back to his cell, purposely interrupting the moment. As he accompanied the burly guard back down the corridor, Rick's feet barely touched the ground.

Back in the office, Zoe's feet did a happy dance beneath her desk.

* * *

Macfarlane and Morgan left the Chatsworth Care Facility and returned to the station. They taxed their antiquated computers for all the processing power they were worth in an effort to learn anything they could about Ollie Perkovich: a new suspect in an old case.

After an hour they gave up. There was no record of the man anywhere. No social security number, no tax returns, no parking tickets.

Morgan mused, "Something's not kosher here."

Macfarlane agreed. "Let's go talk to his girlfriend."

"An excellent idea." Morgan didn't require any excuse to return to Rosey's Tavern. "I'm kinda hungry. Maybe she can comp us again."

They left the station, and on their way to the tavern, placed a call to Teddy Williams.

"Slugger, this is Detective Morgan, LAPD. We have the name and address of the guy that wanted to tear you apart at the restaurant last week. If you still want that restraining order we can get the process started."

"Thank God! I've been afraid to leave my house," said a relieved Teddy.

"You'll be fine," Macfarlane assured him.

A *'thank you'* was followed by a dial tone.

The sun was shining fiercely when the detectives reached Rosey's Tavern. A look around the parking lot told them that the popular eatery was crowded with hungry customers. They found a spot on the far west end of the lot, hiked to the entrance, and made their way inside.

"This place smells so good I think my stomach is about to have an orgasm," moaned Morgan.

"TMI. You know there are some things you can keep to yourself."

A handful of people were seated in the lobby awaiting a table. Morgan looked at the Mickey Mouse watch on his left wrist. "Maybe we can jump this line. Police business."

Macfarlane scanned the tables. "I don't see the Russian, but let's talk to Rosey."

They approached the hostess, showed her their badges, and made their request.

"She's in her office. I'll let her know you're here," said the plucky college freshman behind the lectern.

Morgan's nose caught a whiff of a freshly served entrée and shifted his attention from the hostess to a nearby table. "I think I'll try something new today; maybe a grilled Reuben on rye, although it would be a shame not to sample the meatloaf. I just don't think I'm in a meatloaf mood."

Rosey Kern came out of her office and approached the detectives. When she recognized them, her smile faded.

"You guys again."

"Hello, Ms. Kern. We'd like to ask you a few questions."

A knot suddenly gripped Rosey's stomach. "Let's go to my office."

"We *are* on the waiting list for a table," said Morgan. "Will we be able to hear our name called?"

"Don't worry about it," she reassured him.

Rosey led them through the dining room, past the kitchen, and into a back room where a sign reading 'The Boss' adorned the door. She settled herself behind a desk littered with papers and put a hand through her platinum hair. "What can I do for you boys?"

"What can you tell us about Ollie Perkovich?" asked Macfarlane.

Rosey looked obviously annoyed. "Why? Did Teddy press charges?"

"We're the ones asking the questions," intoned Morgan. "But if you must know, Mr. Williams is not pressing charges, but he *is* in the process of taking out a restraining order."

Rosey was not pleased about that, but if charges *hadn't* been filed, what was the law doing here?

"I don't think he'll bother Teddy anymore. Now, if you'll excuse—"

"How long have you known Mr. Perkovich?" asked Macfarlane.

"About a year."

"He lives with you?" pressed Morgan.

Rosey was beginning to worry. "What's this all about?"

"Where can we find him?" Macfarlane was all but driven at this point.

"Your guess is as good as mine. He's a grown man, and I'm a busy woman with a business to run."

Macfarlane handed Rosey a business card and thanked her for her time. "When you see him, have him give us a call, okay?"

Beads of sweat started to form on Rosey's brow. She really knew very little about her partner and was scared. What the hell had he done now? It had to be bad to have detectives asking all these questions about him.

She stood up, anxious to end this line of inquiry. "Lunch is on me, boys. Have a great day."

"What's good today?" asked Morgan.

"Try the fish and chips. It's todays special."

The detectives stood up. They shook her wet hand, and as soon as they left the room, Rosey took out her cell phone and called Ollie. He picked up on the fourth ring.

"Da?" came the accented voice on the other end.

"Those detectives came back looking for you. What have you done now?"

Ollie was silent for a moment. "What they want?"

"To talk with you. I don't think it has anything to do with Teddy Williams."

Ollie's mind raced. His murder of Tara Potter-Conley-Finley-Goldblatt had been perfect, but now he was a little nervous. He bit his lower lip and drew blood. He recalled that snoopy little bitch Abby asking him a lot of questions at dinner. She had mentioned an old cop who thought that Potter was innocent. Could this be related?

Ollie ended the call. He was in the men's room at the local strip club called 'The Rack.' Though he loved Rosey, he saw nothing wrong with looking at beautiful, naked women. Truth be told, they didn't need to be that attractive. The female form lifted his spirits like worshipers at Church.

Ollie spit out his gum, wiped his bleeding lip with his sleeve, and slammed a fist against a wall. He left the dimness of the club for the brightness of the outside world.

He got in his car, slammed the door, and drove off. Punching the gas as he exited the parking lot, he made a right-hand turn and headed to the local pharmacy.

29
SO LONG, SAM

The old man parked his SUV about a block away from the Chatsworth Care Rehabilitation Facility and opened the tailgate. He put on a wool sweater in the 90-degree heat and eased a blue fedora over his balding skull. He reached into his pocket, pulled out a pair of white gloves, and carefully put them on like a surgeon preparing to operate.

Always the professional, Ollie took few chances. He pulled out his newly purchased walker and slowly inched his way toward the facility. He was chewing his foul smelling gum and taking his time, hoping to blend in with the organized chaos.

Ollie took the cement ramp instead of the four steps to enter the rehab center on this Saturday—the facility's busiest day of the week. Wheelchair-bound residents lined the lobby in their best outfits. Those who were too infirm to leave their rooms, like Sam Beetley in 305E, had their doors open, wishful that family or friends would walk through their doors.

Administrator Letty O'Reily flitted around the lobby greeting guests with a smile that could have sold used cars.

Ollie skirted by the administration office and moved like he knew where he was going. There were three floors to cover, but with many of the rooms empty, and most of the doors open, it didn't take long to traverse the first floor. No troublemaking old detective in view.

He maneuvered his walker to the elevator and pushed the button. The lift took about thirty seconds to descend from somewhere above. It eventually opened with a groan as tired as the residents it transported.

A pair of women in their 90's took another half minute to debark from the space.

Ollie entered the small enclosure and pushed the button for the second floor. He wrinkled his nose at the smell of cheap perfume that could not conceal the scent of urine and sickness. As the doors started to close, a thin-skinned, age-spotted hand stopped the door from closing.

A woman with Lucy-red hair limped inside. "Thanks, sweetie, this elevator takes forever."

Ollie nodded in agreement, being careful to hide his face.

"I'm going to '2' as well."

She looked at the man's face only to see a mouth moving up and down like a jackhammer. Her sight and hearing were in decline, but there was nothing wrong with her sense of smell.

"What is that odor?"

She stepped closer to Ollie and sniffed.

Ollie thought fast. "Sorry. I'm trying to quit smoking and this nicotine gum helps."

The elevator moved like it was running up a hill.

"I've never seen *you* before. Are you new here, or just visiting?"

Ollie didn't want to engage in conversation, but had little choice. "Here to see a friend."

"That's nice. Who's your friend?"

"An old cop. We used to work together."

It just so happened that Ollie's elevator partner, Sharon Hagstrom, was the busybody of Chatsworth Care. She was called an '*ambassador*,' and made it her business to know what was going on around this den of declining health.

"Old cop? He's not on the second floor, I can tell you that."

"It's my first time here. I'm a little confused."

"Join the club."

Finally, the elevator creaked to a stop, its doors opening as slowly as its passengers moved.

Sharon ambled out and turned to Ollie. "Don't be a stranger now." She punctuated her salutation with a widowed smile. "Maybe you can join us for bingo at three o'clock."

"I'll try."

Ollie pushed the button for the third floor. The doors took their time closing.

Sharon looked at Ollie questioningly. "What accent am I hearing?"

Before Ollie could respond, the doors met in the middle with a thud, and the elevator began its slow ascent to the third floor.

"Ye-bat!" muttered Ollie. It was a Russian term for '*fuck*.'

There was no one waiting for vertical transportation when the elevator doors arrived at its destination.

Ollie leaned heavily on his walker and began peering into each room. The sudden sound of gunshots echoing through the hallway caused Ollie to drop to the floor. He reached for a weapon he had not carried in many years.

With the epidemic of mass shootings infecting the country, Ollie assumed it was only a matter of time before some whacko would target a rehab center or nursing home. He lay still until theme music came on and he realized he was reacting to a television show with the volume turned to the max. He sheepishly returned to his feet and reached for his walker.

He continued his quest, going room to room. Most were empty while others had patients lying in beds looking more dead than alive. All rooms had names Scotch taped to their doors. One such door was 305E with the name Beetley printed in an unsteady hand.

Ollie took a quick glance through the opened door and spotted an old man with wispy white hair apparently deep asleep. His TV was tuned to a long canceled cop show that few under the age of 70 would remember. The sound was at full volume, which didn't bother the peeping Tom one bit.

Ollie walked past Sam's room, continued down the hallway, and disappeared around a corner. He stayed in the adjacent corridor for a full five minutes before retracing his steps and returning to Sam's room. He entered and closed the door behind him, stowing his walker against the wall. He lifted the fedora off his head and placed it on a dresser.

He stared at the old detective. Could anyone take this antique seriously, he wondered? For whatever reason, he was sticking his nose in a case that had already been litigated. A verdict had been reached by a jury of his peers and a man was paying the price. The American justice system worked just fine without this meddling old man's help, thank you very much.

If Beetley was running his mouth to that snoopy little twit Abby, there was a chance he could to others as well. The old detective might be in rough physical shape, but his words could be as dangerous as a weapon.

Ollie silently made his way to the side of Sam's bed and picked up a pillow from the vacant bed that shared his room. As he was about to place it over the old man's face, Sam's eyes suddenly opened.

Ollie hesitated for a moment and then slowly stepped towards the helpless old cop.

Sam was very weak. "No," he whispered.

Ollie wasn't moved by Sam's plea. "Goodbye, old timer."

He pressed the pillow over Sam's face and held it firm.

Sam's muffled cries for help were drowned out by a car chase unfolding on television. His legs kicked up, knocking over a tray by the bed and spilling water and applesauce to the floor.

Ollie continued to apply pressure until his opponent lay still. He had put up a pretty good fight, all things considered. The retired detective would pose no more threat.

Ollie removed the pillow and returned it to the other bed. He picked up Sam's limp hand and checked for a pulse that was no longer there. Sam was dead. Perhaps he had done the old guy a favor. Who would want to spend the rest of their days bedridden and wearing diapers?

It was close to lunchtime and Ollie didn't want to linger. He picked up the tray and the empty applesauce container from the floor and set them on the table. Next, he put on his hat and tilted it low over his brow. He collected the walker, closed the door behind him, and slowly made his way to the elevator.

He could hear an arthritis commercial hocking pills on the television as he methodically pushed his walker. It took an eternity for the elevator to arrive, but when it did it was deserted. This time Ollie made it out of the facility without any conversation.

He left the walker by the curb and headed home.

* * *

Kendra was alone in her cell, surrounded by what she considered art, but others considered disturbing. Her physical discomfort had subsided, but her emotional pain grew like Pinocchio's nose. She had dropped over twenty pounds and her skin was beginning to hang like a garment that had lost its elasticity.

"Shitfuck," she said to herself, and to the clowns that surrounded her. She hated her prison job, despised the other inmates, and still had over a year remaining on her sentence.

She took a drag from a cigarette and blew rings of smoke into the air.

* * *

Sam Beetley's body was still warm when Abby walked into his room. He looked peaceful and she wasn't sure if she should disturb him.

"Are you hungry, Sam?"

She stepped closer and smoothed his tussled hair. His stillness alarmed her. She checked for a pulse just as the killer had done. The beat of life had left the room. Sam had worked his last case.

Abby was noticeably shaken as she reached for the phone and notified administrator Letty O'Reily.

"I'm in 305E . . . Mr. Beetley . . . Is . . . Dead."

"Oh my. He was doing so well. I'll send a crew up right away. Stay there until they've finished removing the body."

Abby felt her foot slide on something wet and looked down. Water and applesauce were spilled all over the floor.

Her eyes panned up to the tray on the portable table next to the bed.

She noticed that the water pitcher was perfectly centered, and an empty cup of applesauce lay next to it. A plastic spoon rested neatly inside the cup.

How could the contents have spilled on the floor and look perfect on the table?

As she contemplated that, a two-man team of orderlies wheeled a gurney into the room and placed Sam's lifeless body on it.

Abby couldn't hold back tears that flowed like a faucet. She knew that death was inevitable and common in her future occupation. Perhaps she should rethink her career path.

Letty walked into the room and saw that the young intern was hurting. "It was his time, Honey. He lived a very long and noble life."

Abby nodded. She thought about telling her boss about the spill on the floor, but to what end? So she could spread her conspiracy theory around the rehab center? No, she wouldn't do that, but she would call those two detectives.

"Take the rest of the day off," said Letty in a comforting voice.

Abby didn't have to think twice about that. "Thanks."

She gave Letty a hug and left the room.

* * *

Ollie arrived home and went directly inside. He checked to make sure there was no one else home, then took off his gloves and held them over the stove. They burned like Southern California brush during fire season.

He went into the den and poured himself a healthy amount of a clear spirit. He recounted to himself the intricacies of his dirty deed with remorseless calculation. There was little sign of discomposure, let alone regret. Snuffing Sam was business.

Ollie finished his drink and decided to visit the tavern. He had been avoiding it, but he *was* hungry and in a celebratory mood. It would also provide an alibi should he need one.

He locked the front door, got into his SUV, and started it up. He lit a cigar and took a deep breath before putting the car in gear and driving west.

Detective Morgan, working on his day off, had been staking out Rosey's house for any sign of the Russian. His extracurricular efforts were paying off, and having watched Ollie pull up and enter the house donning white gloves, he now noted the man's bare hands on his departure.

Morgan found that curious. And why was he even wearing them in the first place?

He jotted down the time on a notepad and followed Ollie at a safe distance.

30

HONUS WAGNER
INTERRUPTUS

Detective Macfarlane was spending his day off at a baseball card show. He was an avid fan of the game and loved looking at the cards and photos of his childhood heroes. He passed a booth that featured an autographed photo of Ted Williams and thought about the unfortunate insurance salesman, hoping the woebegone assault victim had followed through with his restraining order.

The off-duty detective picked up a Derek Jeter autographed baseball trapped in a plastic cube and grimaced at the $300 dollar price tag. Why would anybody want to spend that much money on a baseball? While he was pondering the exorbitant price tag, his cell phone sounded.

"Macfarlane."

"Hi detective. It's Abby," came the filtered voice on the other end.

"Hello, Abby. What can I do for you?"

"I wanted to let you know that Sam Beetley died this morning."

Macfarlane's face dropped. "Oh, I'm sorry to hear that," he said in a mildly condolent tone. "He was a good man."

"Yeah, he was. I wouldn't bother you, but I think his death is suspicious."

Macfarlane's eyes narrowed as he moved toward a quieter part of the convention floor. "What makes you think that?"

"Can we talk? In person, I mean."

The detective checked his watch. He was loathe to leave the show before getting a glimpse of a rare Honus Wagner card rumored to be arriving later, but the weight of Abby's words prevailed.

"There's a Starbucks at Zelzah and Chatsworth. Can you meet me there in about an hour?"

Abby said that she would.

*   *   *

Rick Potter was holding court in the rec yard with all the usual suspects.

"I get this job as an assistant editor on a low-budget non-union feature called *Maniac Cop 3*."

"I saw 1 and 2, but never knew they made a third," said Stretch.

"Never heard of it," chimed in Porney."

"You would have liked it," said Swindle. "Some sex in it."

Porney's eyes widened. He made a mental note to view it when he got out.

An older inmate with a long white beard wandered over and joined the group. "Do you gentlemen mind if I join you?"

"Not at all," said Rick. "Have a seat."

The old man sat next to Porney as Rick tried to restore order.

"So, my boss gets fired and they hire the editor that had cut both earlier films to replace him. He had been working on another project, but was now available. The problem was, because he already had his own crew—meaning an assistant and an apprentice—I thought we'd be fired, too."

"Scumbag," muttered Stretch.

"Well, we lucked out. My apprentice was a beautiful young girl who wore hot pants and low-cut blouses to the producer screenings. They didn't want to lose *her* and convinced the new editor into keeping us both."

Porney shifted in his seat.

"We're cutting this classic horror film in a two-bedroom apartment in North Hollywood. We get a call saying that the director wants to see the new editor and me after he's finished the day's shooting."

Rick took a sip of water before continuing.

"We met him and the lead actor at a tequila bar that night and tossed a few back. The director, Bill, was a heavy-set, bald guy that looked more like a wrestler than a movie director. We talked about the film for a while before the editor and actor took off, leaving me alone with Bill. I decided it was time for me to go, as well, but Bill insisted I stay. We ordered another round as a young girl walked over and joined us."

"'Aren't you Bill Lustig, the director?' she asked."

"The guy's eyes lit up like a trick-or-treater hitting the Halloween jackpot."

"As a matter of fact I am."

"The girl slides her seat closer to his. I take this as an opportunity to finally get out of there, but Bill insists that I stay. More drinks arrived and were quickly downed. I was as much a prisoner then as I am now."

"The next thing I know, we're in Bill's jeep singing Neil Diamond songs. He takes us to a karaoke joint and I end up on stage singing Barry Manilow's "*Mandy*" in front of a full house of strangers. I'd never done that before in my life and will never do it again. There's a reason why editors like to work behind the scenes. Anyway, I don't know how I got there, but the next thing I knew I was in the bedroom of our editing suite when my editor and the apprentice walked in the next morning. I was passed out on the bed, with nothing on but one sock and a sheepish smile on my face."

The regulars laughed and started to walk away. The old, bearded inmate tapped Rick on the shoulder. "Thanks for letting me sit in."

"No problem." Rick stuck out a hand. "I'm Rick Potter, ex-film editor. In for murder, but I'm innocent."

"Everyone is, aren't they?" The man smiled and shook his hand. "Pleasure to meet you. Shlomo Koeppel. Rabbi. In for none of your business." Both men chuckled.

Rick took him aside and said, "Rabbi, there's something I'd like to ask you."

* * *

Detective Morgan followed Ollie to Rosey's Tavern. The dark SUV parked in a handicapped space close to the door, and the lone occupant power-walked his way inside.

Parking in a space reserved for the disabled pissed the detective off. If his quarry could do that, what else was he capable of?

Morgan's anger was interrupted by the strains of "*Rap Song*" by the Black Eyed Peas. It was the ringtone he used for his partner's incoming calls.

"Hey."

"Can you meet me at Starbucks in an hour?"

"The one on Chatsworth?"

"Yeah. The one on the northwest corner."

"On my way. I've got some interesting news . . ."

But Macfarlane had already hung up.

Abby was seated in a chair by the window, sipping her Irish Cream Nitro Cold Brew. The weather hadn't cooled down, and the iced coffee gave her a temporary reprieve from the heat.

She gazed out the window that gave her a perfect view of the parking lot. She could see steam rising from the blacktop and couldn't help but notice the inordinate number of BMWs that filled the lot.

When Macfarlane walked in a few minutes later, Abby hardly recognized him. He was dressed casually in jeans and a baseball jersey and looked years younger. She wondered how people could go to work every day dressed in a suit and tie.

He spotted her table and took a seat facing her.

"You look different," said Abby.

"You caught me on my day off."

"I am so sorry. I thought maybe you were working undercover. I hate to bother you, but I thought this was important."

Morgan walked through the door and spotted the pair seated by the window. He was dressed in plaid shorts and a Hawaiian shirt, and resembled a palm tree.

"Sorry I'm late."

He looked at the intern. "Abby. This is a pleasant surprise."

Macfarlane got straight to the point. "We're just getting started. Sam Beetley has passed."

"That's too bad," rued Morgan with casual indifference. "I liked the old fart."

"Abby suspects foul play."

Morgan sat up in his chair like a hung-over barfly who had just been splashed with ice water. He looked straight at Abby. "Talk to us."

Abby wiped an Irish cream mustache off her upper lip before speaking. "I talked with Sam yesterday. He was in good spirits and was looking forward to starting physical therapy next week. I think talk of this murder case somehow invigorated him."

Abby took another sip of her beverage. She noticed that Macfarlane's mustache looked less bushy than she remembered. She had both detectives' undivided attention.

"Do you guys want any coffee?"

"No," replied both detectives simultaneously.

Abby continued. "I came by around noon to see what Sam wanted for lunch. Chatsworth Care offers a choice of two entrees."

"Is the food any good?" interrupted Morgan.

"I've never tried any, but we don't get many complaints. About the food, that is. At first I thought Sam was sleeping, but when I got closer, I realized he was gone."

Macfarlane asked, "What makes you think it wasn't natural causes? He wasn't in the best of health."

"The tray by his bed was perfectly centered on the table," returned Abby without skipping a beat. "On it was a water bottle and an empty applesauce container. Ordinarily, I wouldn't think much of that, but there was a puddle of water and spilled applesauce on the tile floor next to his bed. I could see both accidentally being knocked to the floor, but how could the containers end up back on the table as if nothing happened?"

Abby looked at the officers, trying to gauge their reactions. "Look, Detectives, I may not be schooled in investigating, but someone other than Sam placed those items back on the tray, and I was the only one on duty at that time."

Macfarlane let this sink in. "An autopsy could determine the cause of death."

"They're not going to perform an autopsy on an eighty-five year-old man who was recovering from a stroke," replied Abby.

"A messy floor is not much to go on," said Morgan, stating the obvious.

Macfarlane thought for a moment before speaking. "Are there surveillance cameras at the facility?"

"Of course."

31

GERIATRIC KEYSTONE COPS

The detectives followed Abby to Chatsworth Care like next of kin following a hearse. The lobby was devoid of visitors, who had done their duty earlier in the day and had cleansed their minds of family guilt.

Macfarlane and Morgan entered the administrator's office and scribbled their names on the sign-in sheet.

Letty O'Reily recognized the investigators from their previous visit and gave them her best smile: the one usually reserved for prospective clients. "Good to see you guys again."

She couldn't miss their unusual attire. "Casual Saturday?"

Macfarlane smiled. "We're actually off duty, ma'am, but need a favor."

She smiled back at him and thought he looked kind of cute in his civilian clothes. He reminded her of an out-of-shape middle-aged Tom Selleck. Letty was long divorced and not adverse to seeking companionship. She had no trouble noticing that his ring finger was bare. "How can I help?"

"We need to see security footage from this morning."

Macfarlane turned to Abby. "What time did you discover the body?"

"Around noon. Sam was still warm when I found him."

Macfarlane nodded and looked at Letty. "Say, from ten o'clock to one o'clock."

She took Macfarlane by the hand—a move that did not go unnoticed by his lanky partner—and led the group down an endless hallway to a room marked 'Communications.'

A young man of Hispanic descent, wearing a security badge that displayed his picture and the name Juan beneath it, stood up when the group entered the small enclosure. Behind him was a bank of monitors, all clearly labeled, displaying different views of the facility.

Letty released Macfarlane's hand and directed Juan to rewind the cameras to ten o'clock.

"No problemo."

The monitors began rewinding at less than high speed. The system was antiquated by modern standards, still relying on slow videotape systems, when most businesses had long since gone digital.

Macfarlane turned his attention to the helpful administrator. Holding his hand meant something, didn't it?

He studied her more carefully. They were about the same age in his estimation, although he was no carnival age-guesser attempting to con a buck. She wore makeup that was understated and had fine facial features that reminded him of the sort sculpted into Greek statues. She was dressed professionally, and he liked that her hair was not painted with chemicals.

Juan pushed the stop button and all ten monitors braked to a halt. The time code underneath each monitor read 10:01. He pushed play and the monitors sprang into action, displaying endless footage of visitors coming and going, and patients rolling in their wheelchairs or pushing their walkers. Definitely not riveting viewing.

Morgan smart-alecked, "They ought to put this on cable."

"Can you play it at double speed?" inquired Macfarlane.

Juan pushed another button and the images sped up. It was the fastest many of the residents had moved in years.

Morgan found this funny and started laughing. "It's like watching geriatric Keystone Cops."

Letty frowned. "What are we looking for?"

Macfarlane answered, "Anyone that looks like they don't belong: a stranger in the lobby, or on the third floor. Someone going into Sam Beetley's room."

As the time code numbers tumbled to 11:31, a walker slid into view, pushed across the lobby, past the admittance desk, by a stocky man wearing a low-slung hat. Something about the man caught Macfarlane's attention. He tapped Juan on the shoulder. "Okay, play it at regular speed now."

The walker-assisted 'patient' moved at a snail's pace down the linoleum hallway, peering into each room as he passed by, as if looking for someone. Then he sidled over to the elevator and pushed the button.

Macfarlane asked the administrator if the man looked familiar.

Letty peered closely at the monitor. "I can't get a good look at his face, but I don't think I've seen him before. How about you, Abby?"

Abby studied the screen, shook her head. "I know most of our walker-assisted patients. He's not one of them."

"He's wearing gloves," mused Morgan.

The group continued watching the monitors as the disguised Ollie entered the elevator and disappeared. A moment later an elderly woman joined the stranger in the lift.

"That's Sharon Hagstrom," noted Letty. "She's sharp as a tack."

The tape continued to run for some two minutes, with no sign of movement.

"What happened?" asked Morgan.

"Keep it going a little longer," instructed Letty. "Our elevator isn't going to win any races. It's due for servicing."

They watched as the steel doors finally opened on the second floor. The elderly woman exited the lift and slowly walked off. A couple of minutes later, the man and his walker emerged from the elevator on the third floor. He walked unhurriedly and with apparent great effort as he traversed the hallway.

The assembled group watched as the man paused at the open doorway of one particular room and then continued down the hallway. A short time later he returned and entered the room.

"What room is that?" asked Morgan.

Abby pointed a trembling finger at the monitor. "305E. That's Mr. Beetley's room."

The group had all eyes on an empty hallway. A few minutes later they saw the figure emerge from the room.

Time moved at a turtle's pace as the man made his way to the elevator and eventually disappeared inside it. All eyes shifted to the monitors' marked 'first floor,' as they waited for the door to open. And waited.

"I'd get that serviced sooner than later," noted Morgan.

Eventually, the steel doors separated, and the man and his walker appeared. He tottered through the lobby, briefly stopping at a waist-high trash can next to the entrance. He put his hand to his mouth and deposited something inside it before exiting.

"What did he put in the trash?" asked Abby.

"Let's find out," affirmed Morgan.

The detectives hurried out of the room, with Letty and Abby on their heels. When they reached the lobby, Morgan made a beeline to the trash bin and carried it outside.

After rummaging through discarded tissues, rotten fruit, and paper cups, he found a small wad of pale green gum stuck to a pharmaceutical receipt.

"Bingo."

Abby immediately recognized the pungent odor of the Russian chewing gum. "I know that smell. That's the gum Ollie chews. Yuck."

Morgan wrapped the gum in plastic and stuck it into his pocket.

Macfarlane turned toward the young intern. "Abby, you're a hero."

She started to blush. "Maybe I should pursue a career in law enforcement."

"Let's not get carried away," said Morgan.

Macfarlane turned his attention to the administrator. "Ms. O'Reilly, we really appreciate your help."

"My pleasure." She stepped closer to the casually attired cop. "Here," she said as she thrust a business card into his hand. "If there's anything else I can do for you, just give me a call." She moved even closer to Macfarlane. "Anything at all."

Letty turned and started back to the facility. Macfarlane watched as she entered the building and disappeared from view. His partner nudged him with his elbow and gave him a look.

Abby was observant as well. She smiled and said, "She's really nice . . . And single."

Macfarlane gave an embarrassed grin as he pocketed the card and walked toward his car.

Abby followed the detectives through the parking lot. When they reached Macfarlane's silver Honda CRV, Morgan casually mentioned that he had spent the morning surveilling Rosey and Ollie's house.

Macfarlane gave him a look of surprise.

"Just wanted to see if he was around," announced Morgan.

"And was he was around?"

Morgan pulled out his notebook. "He arrived at the house at 12:35, wearing a hat and gloves. He was inside the house for sixteen minutes and then drove to Rosey's Tavern."

"He wore gloves and a hat? When were you going to tell me this?"

"I got kind of sidetracked," Morgan said defensively.

"Can't you arrest him?" asked Abby.

Macfarlane emitted a lengthy exhale. "It could have been him," he conceded. "The timing is right. But we never got a good look at his face. We need more than that."

"I have a thought," said Morgan. All eyes turned in his direction.

32
LUCKY GETS LUCKY

Noga sat on her bed watching her hamster, Lucky, exercise on a revolving wheel to nowhere. Ever since her visit to the prison Noga had been as quiet as her pet. Seth and Boonsri had tried talking with her, but the six-year-old was mostly uncommunicative. Obviously, taking her to the prison had been a mistake.

Seth knocked on her door and a small voice told him that no one was home.

"Nog, it's Dad. I just want to talk to you."

After a pause, the same small voice said, "Okay, you can come in."

Seth opened the door and took a seat next to her on the bed. He followed her eyes to her pet.

"I don't want Lucky in that cage anymore."

"Lucky is a pet, Nog. I don't know if she'd survive outside on her own."

"She didn't do anything wrong, and I have her in a cage like Grandpa. It's not fair," she protested.

Seth let that sink in before answering. His daughter was wise beyond her years.

"Sometimes life isn't fair, sweetheart. I don't know why that is, but I know it's true."

"I don't want to go to that jail anymore," she persisted.

Seth put an arm around her. "I shouldn't have taken you. You're too young."

"It's not your fault, I wanted to go. Now, I want to let Lucky loose."

Noga put her head on his shoulder and began to weep. Seth held her tight. "It's okay to cry. We can let Lucky go if you really want to."

Noga nodded her head as they sat together watching Lucky exhaust her furry body on its circular treadmill. Seth dabbed at the moisture that was forming in his own eyes. He hugged his daughter until Boonsri called them to dinner.

*   *   *

Kendra was depressed: clinically so. She had lost more weight and was as uncommunicative as a little girl weighing the fate of a caged hamster. Her friend June had given up trying to help her, and now she was truly alone in a facility that housed over 1,600 offenders. Some people just can't be helped.

She lay on her cot surrounded by the clown art that lined her cell like grotesque, circus-themed wallpaper. She thought of all the shit she'd been through, which only deepened her depression.

"Shitfuck."

She was in no condition to make life-altering decisions but decided to pay a visit to Alberta (aka "Big Al") anyway. Big Al was one of the tougher inmates at CCWF, and the best tattoo artist in the joint. Big Al had fashioned a tattoo machine from broken spoons and deodorant labels, and used burnt ash for ink. She was considered a celebrity among the inmates and her services were very much in demand.

The canvas that was Kendra's skin already had several tattoos— some professionally applied—but most were prison body art from her earlier incarceration. However, her ass was a clean slate, so she thought adding a couple there would be cool. She had no money for the prison artist, but had her body to trade.

Big Al liked women, and Kendra could deal with that.

* * *

Paul and Madonna were in their home studio putting down vocal tracks on a new song when his cell phone rang.

"Shit. That ringtone doesn't work with this tune," Paul quipped with irritation.

"Just answer it," said Madonna.

He snatched the phone from its perch on his keyboard. "Hello? Yes, it's Paul. Oh. Now?"

He looked at Madonna whose eyebrows arched.

"Okay." He clicked off the phone.

"What was that about?"

"Those detectives I spoke with last week want to come by and talk some more. They'll be here in half an hour."

Madonna's interest perked up. "What do you think it's about?"

"Well, it's either about dad, or a four-month-old speeding ticket."

The detectives arrived exactly 30 minutes later.

Paul let them in and led them downstairs to the guest quarters that he and Madonna shared. He motioned the cops to the couch while Madonna tried discreetly to move the bong that was stationed on the coffee table like a billboard asking to be read. Both cops noticed, but said nothing.

Morgan, who fancied himself as somewhat of an amateur interior decorator, glanced around the room. "I like your choice of furniture: a very bold statement. And the red accent wall is a nice touch."

Madonna smiled. "Thanks. I call it early Goodwill."

Macfarlane turned serious and got right to the point. "Mister Potter, we have been thinking about what you told us last week.

That you watched your dad leave the victim's residence and heard his ex-wife screaming at him."

"It's the truth, I swear to God."

Morgan chimed in. "We believe you."

His senior partner continued. "We have a thought we'd like to run by you. It's unorthodox—and dangerous."

His words piqued Paul's attention.

Macfarlane exchanged glances with his partner before continuing. "Are you familiar with a man named Ollie Perkovich?"

Morgan jumped in. "He lives with Rosey Kern, Nate's mother-in-law."

"I know who he is, kind of looks like that old actor Peter Lorre."

Morgan smiled at his partner. "See, even this kid knows who that is."

Macfarlane chose to ignore the remark and continued on with Paul. "We shouldn't tell you this, but we have reason to believe that he could be involved with Tara Potter—"

"Conley-Finley-Goldblatt's murder." Morgan finished his sentence.

Paul and Madonna listened intently.

Macfarlane glanced petulantly at his partner and then continued. "We also believe that he may have been responsible for a retired detective's death last Saturday morning."

"We don't have enough to arrest him, and if we bring him in for questioning he could end up running," added Morgan.

Macfarlane got to the point. "Mr. Potter . . . Paul. What we'd like you to do is wear a wire and confront this Perkovich. Tell him what you told us. That you were there the night of the murder and that you saw your dad come out of the house with Tara yelling at him. Tell him the words that she called out."

Morgan took over. "No one else knows that, so he'll *know* you were there. We'd also like you to mention Detective Beetley's murder."

Paul's head turned from one detective to the other like a fan at a tennis match.

Macfarlane said, "If we're right, he may try to pay you off—"

"Or kill you," interjected Morgan.

Macfarlane made a face and turned to his partner. "We'll be nearby in any case."

Paul didn't have to think twice.

"I'm all in."

Madonna shifted closer to Paul and held his hand. To the detectives she said, "Can I get you something to eat?"

Morgan grinned from ear to ear. He had never turned down a free meal.

33
FREE AT LAST

Noga awoke early, brushed her teeth, and got dressed. She then outfitted her Beach Barbie, changing the doll's bikini from pink to blue. Even dolls needed to mix it up now and then.

Noga sat on the edge of her bed, staring at her pet hamster. Lucky was sleeping, having exhausted her little body by running in circles.

"You've been a good friend, Lucky. I want you to be happy. You're not supposed to be locked up like this."

Lucky opened an eye and yawned. Her little nose twitched as if she understood.

"C'mon, let's go."

Noga picked up the small cage and carried it to the kitchen. Seth was on his second cup of coffee after downing a hearty helping of French toast. He saw his daughter holding the cage.

"Are you sure you want to do this, sweetheart?"

Noga nodded and tried hard not to tear up. She was a big girl now.

Boonsri looked on as Seth carried Lucky's cage, with Noga at his side. They exited the front door and opened the side gate that led to what they called '*the back forty*.'

The Potter estate was three stories with a backyard lush with vegetation. The landscaping had cost a fortune many years ago, when Rick and Cheryl had it installed back when they were making major renovations to the house and property, but the upkeep had been too expensive to maintain. Now the yard was overgrown with untrimmed trees and knee-high weeds.

Seth had no idea if Lucky would be able to survive, but admired his daughter's decision to set the hamster free.

They reached the bottom of the hill and Noga opened the cage door. Lucky saw the open space but remained still.

"That's okay, Lucky. You can go. Be happy. Have puppies."

She held on to her Beach Barbie like a parishioner clutches a rosary. Lucky took a couple of tentative steps towards freedom. She looked up at Noga, twitched her hamster nose, and took off running.

Father and daughter looked on as Lucky disappeared into thick ivy and dandelion weeds. Noga waved to her pet as Seth took hold of her hand.

"Good-bye, Lucky," she whispered in a halting voice as she brushed a tear from her eyes.

*   *   *

Kendra was sore from being punctured over and over by a scary lesbian tattoo artist. It hurt like hell, but she thought it was worth the pain. She had instructed Big Al to put the word '*Thoughts*' on one cheek and the word '*Prayers*' on the other. She needed both.

She had paid for the tattoo with sex, and it hadn't been as bad as she'd thought. Big Al was not fond of Kendra; nobody was. But this had been a business transaction, so any animosity was put aside. Besides, Kendra was not bad looking for a skinny skank.

Now the only thing she had to worry about was contracting hepatitis or AIDS. Blood-born pathogens transmitted from unclean needles and ink sources contributed to the risk.

Tattooing in prison was forbidden, but the system generally turned a blind eye towards the practice, which was rampant in the penal system.

*   *   *

A half-filled parking lot suggested that it was past the dinner rush when the police van pulled up across the street from Rosey's Tavern. Paul was wearing a long sleeved work shirt and blue jeans. It was impossible to detect the listening device that was strapped around his torso.

Morgan glanced out the window and espied Ollie heading into the tavern. "Get ready. He's entering the premises."

Macfarlane turned to Paul. "Okay, let's go over this again."

Paul's adrenaline was flowing. "All right. I go into the bar, get a seat as close to this asshole as I can, and order a drink. I make casual conversation with the creep and drop the bomb that I followed my dad to Tara's place the night of the murder. That I waited for him and heard Tara screaming, '*You'll never prove it, asshole.*' I get the guy to go outside with me. And then you guys better be all over him like ticks on a rhino."

"Don't worry about us. We'll be there," said Morgan as he reached into a bag of sour cream and onion flavored chips. "How does the wire feel?"

Uncomfortable as hell. Like everything else."

"That's normal," said Macfarlane. "And drink something light. We don't want you drunk and getting sloppy. On second thought, just pretend to drink."

"Got it. I'll try not to kill the motherfucker."

"That would not be good," agreed Morgan as he reached in for another potato chip.

Paul undid his seatbelt. "Okay, let's do this."

He took a deep breath and climbed out of the van. He looked back to the cops. "I hope you guys know what you're doing," as the door slammed shut.

* * *

Kendra and a dozen or so fellow inmates were in the communal showers trying to wash away the stink of incarceration. All modesty was rendered mute when one entered prison. She noticed others looking her way and giggling. She didn't think much of it and thought perhaps they were admiring her new tats.

June was nearby and glanced over at her old friend. When Kendra turned, June got a good look at her behind.

"Oh no."

June walked over to Kendra. "I see you got some new ink."

"You looking at my ass? What do you think?"

"I'm not sure it's in good taste."

"What's wrong with '*Thoughts*' and '*Prayers*?'"

"Well . . . Nothing . . . Except" . . . "

"Except what?" Kendra was starting to lose her patience.

June took her by the hand and led her to a nearby full length mirror, where Kendra could look over her shoulder and get a good view of her posterior. Her face contorted when she saw one cheek prominently reading '*Shit*' in bold, gothic lettering. The other cheek read '*Fuck*.'

Kendra's eyes bulged in disbelief. "Shitfuck!"

34
POETIC JUSTICE

Paul strolled into the restaurant as casually as a man in his tenuous position could. All of his senses were heightened. Savory smells invaded his nostrils and the steady murmur of voices filled his ears.

He walked toward the bar and saw Ollie sitting on a stool conversing with his brother Nate, who was stationed behind the bar. Empty chairs surrounded his subject.

Nate's expression turned into an ugly sneer when he noticed Paul approaching, but there was nothing he could do about it. His brother was a customer in a public restaurant and Nate was just a hired hand working for close to minimum wage and tips.

Paul returned the sneer with a smile and took the vacant seat next to Ollie, who was chewing gum and holding a large tumbler of clear liquid in his right hand. Paul spied a crinkled-up blue gum wrapper on the oak surface of the bar, unaware of its significance.

"What the fuck do you want?" grumbled Nate.

Paul wasn't surprised at the animosity in his brother's tone—they hadn't spoken in years. "You need to work on your people skills. I don't think that's the proper greeting for a paying customer."

Inside the van, Detective Morgan laughed out loud. "I love this kid."

"Coors Light," Paul said with a smile to his estranged brother.

Paul ordered the watered down Pilsner because in the old days it had been the family joke. Rick thought the beer tasted like tainted water from Flint, Michigan, and had banned it from the house.

Nate was not amused. He picked up a schooner and walked to the beer station, which had a handful of brews on tap. He filled the glass halfway and slammed it on the counter in front of his brother.

Paul noticed the inadequate pour. "I guess I'm one of those guys that looks at a glass as half-empty."

"You're lucky you got anything at all," said Nate as he moved to the other end of the bar.

Paul lifted the schooner, took a sip, and turned to his target. "I like how this place makes you feel welcome."

There was no response. Ollie kept his head down and nursed his drink.

Paul leaned in towards the stolid Ollie. "Say, I think . . . I know you, don't I?"

Ollie didn't bother to look up. He kept his eyes locked on his drink. "I don't think so."

Paul leaned in a little closer, lowered his voice, eyeing Ollie closely. "Sure, you remember, don't you? My dad was holding a napkin to his face, and Tara was screaming, '*You'll never prove it, asshole.*'"

Paul smiled grimly at the squat figure seated beside him. "Ring a bell?"

Those words hit Ollie like an uppercut to the jaw. How could this punk possibly know that? The fact was that he *had* seen Rick leaving with the makeshift bandage on his face, and *had* heard Tara's words. What he didn't understand was, if this guy *was* there that night, why hadn't he said anything to the police? Why was he doing this now?

Ollie turned away and sipped his drink. "I don't know what you're talking about."

"I saw you go into her house just after my dad left." He leaned closer to Ollie, as if conveying a dark secret. "The next morning she was found murdered."

"I'm warning you. Do not fuck with me."

Nate watched from the end of the bar as he squeezed a lime into a frozen margarita. *What could they possibly be talking about?*

Paul was not put off by the threat. He raised his voice and said, "If you'd like, we can talk about the death of an old detective in a rehab facility, as well. You've been a busy little shitbag, haven't you? Shall we tell Nate what you did to his mother?"

The mention of Beetley was like a knockout punch. If he had been a boxer in the ring, he would have fallen to the canvas. He instantly knew that it had to have been Abby who was causing this trouble. She had asked questions and spoke about the detective at the family dinner. His mind replayed Sam's murder. He had gone to the facility in disguise and worn gloves. There was no way they could connect him with the old man's death.

One thing was sure; as soon as he dealt with Nate's brother he would turn his attention to that talky little bitch, Abby. Then he would return to his homeland and disappear.

He glared at Paul with murder in his eyes. "What do you want?"

"I have a list. Where shall I begin?"

Morgan chuckled again inside the police van. "This kid is a natural."

Ollie finished his drink before responding. "Not here."

Paul didn't know enough to be frightened. In fact, he was enjoying this. "Fine, let's go for a walk."

Ollie slid off the stool and stood up on sturdy legs. Whatever he was drinking had no effect.

Paul did the same and placed a twenty-dollar bill on the counter. He shouted to Nate, "Keep the change, barkeep."

Nate watched as Ollie and Paul left the building together. *What was this all about?*

Inside the van, Macfarlane and Morgan were watching, too. "Get ready to move," said the mustache to the cop behind the wheel.

The odd pair exited the tavern and walked off in a southerly direction down the boulevard, like two old friends on an evening stroll. The air had cooled considerably and a full moon was beginning to rise in the eastern sky.

Macfarlane viewed the two men through his binoculars like a birdwatcher tracking a rare species. "Start the engine."

Paul and Ollie turned a corner onto a darkened side street. Ollie stopped to light a cigar, then continued walking. "You want money? I'm not a wealthy man."

"I'm not greedy. First, I'm curious why you killed her."

"I never killed anybody. I'm a retired plumber."

Paul stopped and looked down at the Russian. "Fine. You want to play games? I'll go to the cops. They might find this very interesting." He turned and started to walk away.

Ollie put his hand on the taller man's shoulder. "Wait . . . Okay, let's talk."

The two adversaries continued their 'stroll.' A dangerous cat-and-mouse game was taking place here, and Paul wondered how this was all going to play out. He hoped the cops were catching all of this.

Ollie's hand slid into his jacket pocket where he kept a switchblade.

The unmarked police van crept along two blocks behind them with lights off. Macfarlane tracked their every step.

"You should thank me," Ollie quipped. "It was Tara who shot your mother."

Paul stopped in his tracks, staring wide-eyed at the Russian national. Nate's wife Kendra had spent a decade and a half in the slammer for that crime.

"A strange twist of fate, no?" Ollie waited for his words to sink in before continuing. "I don't know why she did it, and I don't give a shit. But Kendra served *her* time and it broke my Rosey's heart. I had to kill her. It was justice."

Paul found himself struggling to stay focused. "Perhaps she deserved to die, but now *my* dad is serving *your* time."

Inside the van, Macfarlane asked, "You get all that?"

Morgan nodded. "Clear as a bell."

"Let's move. Now!"

The van sped up.

Ollie and Paul were now on a particularly dark section of the street. Ollie's hand was in his coat pocket, clutching the knife.

Paul looked around at the dark, isolated surroundings and sensed danger. "Wait a minute. I'm not going any further. You must think I'm stupid."

"Yes, I do. Typical American."

Ollie pulled out the knife and the blade sprang to life with the spontaneity of a teenaged boy reading a *Playboy* magazine.

The van turned right, tires squealing in protest.

Paul tried to take a step backward, but Ollie was strong and had grabbed him by his shirt. A quick swipe ripped through the material, finding skin and wire. Blood started to ooze.

Paul took a wild swing at his assailant, but Ollie was quick and experienced in matters of close combat. He moved in, thrust his arm, and found more skin.

Paul clutched at his shoulder and wondered where the hell the cops were.

"Over there," Macfarlane pointed.

The driver floored it, burning rubber in the process.

Ollie was startled by the sound and turned. When he did, Paul took a swing that grazed the stocky man's ear.

Ollie was infuriated, like a rabid animal. He lifted the blade to finish Paul off when a shot sounded from somewhere behind them.

Ollie went down like a sack of potatoes, blood spurting in all directions. Morgan's shot had struck him in the head.

The killer had been killed.

Macfarlane rushed to Paul and helped him up. "You all right?"

Paul opened his shirt, checked his wounds, streaming with blood. "I don't know. I think so. Did you get all that?"

Macfarlane smiled. "It's on tape. Let's get you to the ER."

Paul smiled weakly as Macfarlane escorted him to the van.

"Get him to the hospital right away," the detective instructed the driver.

A siren sounded and the van sped away.

Morgan took out a handkerchief, picked up the switchblade from the ground, and placed it in a plastic evidence bag. He looked down at the lifeless form below him.

The back of Ollie's head was scattered about the pavement. Macfarlane walked over to his partner.

"That was some shooting, Randolph. You just saved that kid's life."

Morgan took the compliment in stride. "Just doing my job. I used to be Special Ops in Afghanistan."

Macfarlane gave him a quizzical look. "You never told me that before."

Morgan shrugged. "Can I ask you something?"

"Sure," said his partner.

"I don't know about you, but I'm starving. Would it be in bad taste to grab a bite at the tavern?"

Macfarlane gave the notion two seconds of consideration. "You just killed the owner's boyfriend. What do *you* think?"

"Too soon? I am craving meatloaf."

35

HOME SWEET HOME

FOUR MONTHS LATER

The usual suspects were gathered around Rick Potter, listening intently to another Hollywood story.

"And then I opened the door to the storage room and found my assistant down on her knees pleasuring the director."

The group wasn't surprised. "Doesn't that sort of thing happen all the time in Hollywood?" inquired Swindle.

"It never happened to me," explained Rick.

"Too bad," said Porney. "Your assistant sounds talented."

Rabbi Koeppel, who had become a member of the group, muttered, "Oy gevalt."

"Listen guys, I'm kind of anxious to get out of here."

"Just a couple more?" pleaded Stretch.

They knew that this would be the last of Rick Potter's stories. Their friend was dressed in blue jeans and a flannel shirt that hung loose on his svelte frame. He was about to exit the California State Prison, Corcoran, after having been exonerated by the state. It had taken time to pass through the judicial system, but with the new evidence provided by Sam Beetley's gum wrappers, Paul's statement to the police, the recorded comments provided on the wired tape conversation, and the attempted murder of Paul, the appeals court had agreed that there was sufficient material to proceed with a re-hearing of the case against Pick Potter. And this time, a jury of Rick's peers had found in his favor, and the courts finally ordered that he be set free.

Rick was getting antsy to start his new life. "Okay, one more story and then I'm gone with the wind."

No one got his movie reference.

"This time let me tell you a baseball story. It's the late 70s. My best friend John was a sports reporter covering the California Angels. He takes me to a Yankee game because that's my favorite team."

"I hate the fucking Yanks," announced Stretch Beresford. "Go Sox."

"I may have to reevaluate our friendship." Rick continued, "The Angels win the game and John says that he needs to go to the Angels' locker room to get quotes for tomorrow's paper. He then asks me to do the same in the Yankee clubhouse. I'm overjoyed, like a little kid. I get to mingle with the Yanks. Then he tells me to talk to Reggie Jackson and ask him how it felt to strike out four times in a game: the fucking golden sombrero for heaven's sake. Now I know he's not going to be too happy to talk about his performance, but it was my assignment."

"Jesus Christ," exhaled the Rabbi.

"Jesus Christ is right," agreed Rick. "I had press credentials, a pen and paper, and entered the visitors' clubhouse."

"The players were in various stages of showering or getting dressed and talking to reporters: real reporters, not just a fan who scored a free ticket like me. I scan the room and spot Reggie sitting in front of his locker. He's stark naked and all alone. The other journalists knew better than to approach him after a game like that. So, I take a deep breath and walk over to the future Hall of Famer. I politely request if I can ask him a few questions. He looks at me like I just vomited, but nods his head in the affirmative. We gab for about ten minutes and he really opens up. He tells me that he has to forget about this game, that tomorrow he may get four hits. He says that things even out in baseball and in life. I was the only one to talk with him. John was thrilled."

His friends laughed and Rick took it in.

He looked at this strange group of eccentrics and knew that he would miss them. Perhaps one day they could all gather together on the outside and share a bottle of the good stuff.

Guard Hinkle came by to escort the ex-convict to freedom. "Warden wants to see you before you leave."

Rick nodded and hugged his pals' goodbye. As he walked away, he heard Stretch call to him. "Rick."

Rick turned and looked back. "What?"

Stretch grinned. "You oughtta write a book."

"Thanks. Maybe I will." He smiled back at his soon to be ex-cellmate and continued walking.

He followed Hinkle to the elevator and down the familiar corridors to Goldberg's office. He got hoots and well wishes from those that would be left behind.

Rick entered the outer office and saw Zoe sitting behind that huge desk. She looked up at him and smiled. This was a vision he would always remember. Her presence had helped give him hope, and he would miss her most of all.

She stood up and put her arms around him. "I knew you were innocent, I can always tell."

"Annyeonghaseyo, Zoe."

"Annyeonghaseyo, Rick."

Zoe kissed him on the cheek as the older man held her tight.

"I'm almost sorry to see you go," whispered Zoe.

"I'm going to miss you," replied Rick. He then released his hold on Zoe and walked stoically through the connecting door.

Goldberg was finishing up a phone call. "Tuesday is fine, see you at three."

He hung up the phone and extended a hand. "So, leaving us so soon?"

"I guess I'm rehabilitated."

The warden turned to a file cabinet and opened a drawer. He withdrew a golden bottle of single malt Scotch and poured the liquid into two glasses.

"To your future. You now have one."

"Ganbei," said Rick using the Chinese term for toasting. "I'll drink to that."

And each did.

"I trust that you'll stay out of trouble. I don't want to see you again unless we do a film together."

"I'm almost finished with your script. I'll send you my notes when I'm done."

The warden became serious. "And if you don't mind, perhaps you can find me a literary agent—and not at a small agency, either. This script is high concept material."

The two men shook hands for a second time, and Rick exited the warden's office.

Zoe heard the interior door open and looked up. "What will you do now?"

"Two minutes ago I would have said I was going to have a nice sip of Scotch, but the warden has crossed that off my immediate bucket list. I don't really know. Go back to LA; be with my kids for a while. Maybe sue the city, or go back to Shanghai. I have no idea."

Zoe said, "Don't forget me." She stepped closer.

"Not a chance," whispered Rick.

They gazed into each other's eyes like they do in the movies. He then kissed her on the lips ... A passionate kiss that suspended time.

"Hey, get a room," quipped Hinkle. This time there was a grin on his huge mug.

They ended their embrace and Zoe retrieved a small box that contained the possessions Rick had carried with him when he entered the joint: a wallet, cell phone, belt, and some loose change.

She handed him the small container. "You may want this."

"Thanks." He pecked her on the lips, looked into her eyes, and left the office with Hinkle by his side. Zoe watched him walk away. With each step forward he left the past behind.

When they reached the outer perimeter of the barbed-wire barrier, Rick stopped and turned to the guard.

"Hinkle, I'd like to thank you."

"Thank me for what?"

"Well—for not beating me to a pulp, for starters."

Hinkle laughed. "Hey, if you needed it, you woulda got it." Then he softened. "Seriously, I have just one question for you."

"Shoot." Rick cringed at his choice of words.

"Do you think I could make it in Hollywood as an actor?"

The man was serious.

"It's possible. You do have a unique look. If I was you, and I'm glad I'm not, I'd take a couple of acting classes. It's not as easy as it looks."

Hinkle stuck out his boxing glove of a hand. "Stay out of trouble."

Rick stepped out of COR with the feeling only a man who has been unjustly cooped up in prison and suddenly finds himself a free man knows. The air smelled fresher, the colors more vibrant. He looked around and spotted Paul and Madonna waiting for him by Paul's F-150.

She ran up to him and threw her arms around him. "Thank God, you're free."

Rick smiled. "Yeah, thank God." He had never believed in the concept before, but was now open to the possibility of a higher power.

Paul joined them and they held each other like they had won the lottery. And in a way they had.

"Let's go home," said Paul.

"Yeah, let's do that before they change their minds," joked Rick. His voice unexpectedly cracked, as a tear cascaded down his cheek like morning dew.

For Rick, the ride home was amazing. He stared out the window at the vast expanse of almond groves and strawberry fields and appreciated them for the first time.

Paul filled him in on what had transpired to arrange his freedom. He told him of Detective Beetley who had given his life to find out the truth. He spoke glowingly of the two Devonshire Division detectives that had made it all happen. Of Madonna, who insisted he tell the detectives all he knew. And of his knife fight with the late Ollie Perkovich.

"Did that bastard cut you bad?" asked Rick.

"I'll have a scar, but Madonna thinks it's sexy."

Madonna smiled and rubbed her hand over Paul's chest. "I do." She turned and gave Rick a playful wink.

There was not a lot of talking the rest of the trip home. Rick rode south on I-5 surrounded by his loving family.

Billboards were posted along the flat and boring stretch of highway leading to the Los Angeles suburb of Northridge. Rick had traveled this road many times, but was discovering these signs for the first time.

"Save water"

"Almonds use too much water"

"Owens Valley saves the farms"

"The End is near"

"Dump Trump!" (A giant American flag, with the slogan 'Make America Great Again' emblazoned over it).

Rick mused to himself. *One man's sorrow is another man's dream.*

The taste of freedom was sweet, and Rick planned to savor it the rest of his life. There was just one sad thought to allay his happiness, one additional touch to keep his new life from perfect. He thought back to the beautiful lady Zoe, whose humor and sensitivity and gentle ways had buoyed his spirits during his final weeks in

Corcoran. The thought of never seeing her again was going to leave an empty spot in his heart, for a long, long time to come.

When they arrived at the Northridge house, Seth, Boonsri, and Noga were sitting on the porch waiting for them. Upon seeing her grandpa, Noga screamed with the delight of someone her age. She ran to Rick and hugged him around his knees.

"I love you, Grandpa!"

Rick bent down and said, "*Ikh bin azoy tsufridn. Ikh hab dir lib.*"

Noga squeezed him tighter.

Seth looked at his father in disbelief. "Since when did you learn *Yiddish?*"

"There was a rabbi in the next cell block who taught me a couple of phrases."

Seth grinned. "What does it mean?"

Boonsri answered for him. "It means I'm so happy. I love you."

The sun was setting into a collage of dusky pinks and purples as the reunited family entered the house.

Rick settled into the guest room where a bottle of the good stuff was waiting for him, begging to be opened.

He poured the elixir into a crystal glass and sat on a bed with a real mattress. His nightmare had ended. He reached over and removed his wallet from the box, wondering if it contained any money. When he opened it, a slip of paper fell to the bed. He picked it up and saw the name "Zoe" and a phone number written in a delicate hand. He wasted no time calling it.

In a fourth story single apartment in the quiet farm belt town of Corcoran, California, a phone rang. A hand picked up on the first ring. "Hello?"

"Annyeonghaseyo," said Rick.

Zoe's heart skipped a beat.

"Miss me?" Rick continued.

"Who is this?" Zoe asked, mischievously.

Rick laughed. "Has it been that long?"

Zoe joined his laughter. "I'm just joking. And yes, as a matter of fact, I do miss you."

They talked for close to an hour about everything from books and politics to sports and love. When Rick finally hung up the phone, he poured another drink and thought, "What could be better than this?"

He was about to find out.

36

THERE IS A GOD

That night, on an occasion that was Thanksgiving and Christmas rolled into one, the reunified Potter clan gathered around the dinner table and feasted on a Boonsri-Noga Thai concoction. Linda Ronstadt's angelic voice filled the house with chants of "*Long, Long, Time.*" If one didn't know better, this could have been any family at peace with the world, showing no signs of the dysfunction that had plagued them for so many years. Boonsri had even allowed her father-in-law into her private sanctuary, the kitchen, to cut some vegetables.

When the peach cobbler was down to crumbs, the doorbell sounded.

"I'll get it," said Rick. "I can use the exercise."

Rick walked to the door and was taken aback to see Nate standing there. His son looked older—and sad. They eyed each other for an uncomfortable beat before Nate stammered, "I heard you were out." Rick didn't know where this conversation was headed.

After another brief and awkward silence, Nate tried to continue. "Dad, I . . . "

Rick didn't need to hear any more. He hugged his son like he had when Nate was little. Tears flowed freely from both their eyes.

"I'm so sorry, dad. For everything."

"That's okay, son."

They released from their hug and wiped their eyes.

Nate had more to say. "Do you think . . . Can we . . . Start over? Have it be like it used to be?"

"I've been dreaming of this moment for a long time. Come in. You'll have to make peace with your brothers."

Nate nodded as father and son walked into the house.

Paul called out, "Who was that?" A moment later he had the answer to his question.

When they all saw Nate the room fell silent. Paul stood up to face him. After a brief an awkward silence Nate extended his hand and Paul shook it.

"I guess I've been kind of a jerk," said Nate in a voice that quivered with emotion.

"What do you mean, kind of?" Paul replied, before he replaced the handshake with a hug.

Seth got up and joined his brothers. "Welcome back." He then introduced his big brother to the rest of the family. Noga showed her uncle her Beach Barbie Doll and insisted that he sit next to her. Boonsri asked if he was hungry and Nate wasn't shy.

"I'm starving."

Thomas Wolfe wrote, "You can't go home again." In this case he was mistaken. For the next hour a family was reborn. It was perfect.

When it was over, the brothers all exchanged another round of jubilant bear hugs. The years of alienation evaporated like the alcohol in their glasses.

Rick walked Nate to his beat up old truck.

Nate lingered at the door. "I want you to know that I'm divorcing Kendra. She's been bad news from the beginning: I just never saw it coming." Nate was no actor: his words came directly from the heart. Tears dripped down his chin and onto his shirt.

Father and son hugged again, and Rick watched Nate's truck round a corner and vanish into the night. He had started back to the house when he heard rustling in the ivy.

Rick bent down to take a look. A pair of beady eyes stared back at him, then hopped in his direction.

"What have we here?"

A hamster named Lucky nuzzled at his shoe. He picked up the small rodent and carried it inside the house. Seth said to his dad, "Man, this has been an amazing night." He noticed that Rick carried something in his hands. "What you got there?"

"I'm not sure. I found this little guy rooting around in the ivy."

Noga took a look and jumped with joy. "Lucky! It's Lucky! She's come home!"

Rick transferred the furry animal to his granddaughter. They all watched as Noga hugged her hamster like she'd never let her go.

* * *

At the Central California Women's Facility in Chowchilla, inmate Kendra Potter lay on her cot with night sweats, surrounded by her clown paintings that seemed to be staring at her with a distorted look of disgust. From a nearby cell an out of tune kazoo warbled a carnival melody.

Her throat was sore, and a skin rash that had broken out on her butt and spread to her back itched like a son–of–a–bitch. Kendra had been ill for a few days now and had spent a night in the infirmary where blood had been taken. Something was definitely wrong. She kept muttering "shitfuck" over and over like an idiot savant.

No one gave a rat's ass.

The prison doctor approached her cell and asked her how she was doing.

"How do you think I'm doing for God sake?"

He sat down next to her and placed an arm around a boney shoulder. "I'm afraid I have some bad news."

Kendra's blood began to boil. "Well, I'll be damned."

And she was.

ACKNOWLEDGEMENTS

Writing this book, the third in the trilogy, required help. I am fortunate to have so many talented friends who volunteered their time to make this novel better.

I couldn't have done it without the help of Randy Morgan, award-winning film editor, screenwriter, and close friend, who tirelessly gave me notes like a worried director viewing his first cut.

The same goes to David Koeppel, a terrific film editor and storyteller who kept me on point. Both of you helped more than you know.

Jimmy Huston took hours out of his schedule to assist me with this book. The kindness of strangers. Thank you so much.

Randy Wiles was the first to read an early draft of *Well, I'll be Damned*. His encouragement and suggestions were incorporated within the pages.

ABOUT THE AUTHOR

As a Primetime Emmy Award winning film editor for the "Loves Labor Lost" episode of *ER,* Rick has been telling stories on film for years. In his spare time he enjoys traveling to exotic locals, watching his beloved Yankees, and sipping single malt Scotch.

Well, I'll be Damned is the final chapter in the Rick Potter trilogy that began with *Should Have Seen it Coming* and continued with *Just My F***ing Luck.* He lives in Granada Hills, California with his wife Shirley and two of his adult children.